TH

MW01623973

VOWS

DANIEL HURST

www.danielhurstbooks.com

Copyright © 2021 by Daniel Hurst

All rights reserved.

No part of this book may be reproduced in any form or by an electronic or mechanical means, including information storage or retrieval systems, without written permission from the author, except for the use of brief quotations in a book review.

This is a work of fiction. Names, characters, businesses, places, events, locales, and incidents are either the products of the author's imagination or used in a fictitious manner. Any resemblance to actual persons, living or dead, or actual events is entirely coincidental.

PROLOGUE

My wedding day consisted of the usual things one would expect on such an occasion. There were beautiful bouquets of flowers everywhere, whether they were in the hands of bridesmaids or sitting in vases in the centre of all the tables. There were smart suits and stylish dresses and plenty of champagne and canapes too. And there were speeches; some emotional, some funny, but all of them warming the hearts of those who heard them.

It was a traditional wedding in every sense.

The vows were traditional too.

My husband and I had considered writing our own vows for the big day, imprinting our personality on the proceedings instead of just saying the same things that everybody says when they stand in front of their family and friends and pledge their commitment to each other. But in the end, we decided that we were going to stick to tradition and recited the vows that most people in society know and understand.

For better, for worse.

For richer, for poorer.

In sickness and in health.

Those vows are very simple, and so they should be. They say everything that a loving couple need them to say. I know I was committed to honouring them, and I believed the man standing opposite me at the altar was committed to doing the same.

But I was wrong.

The man I married that day has broken each and every one of those vows.

That's why I could never forgive him.

It's also why I had to have my revenge.

1

ALISON

I fiddle with the wedding ring on my left hand as I wait to be called into my appointment, and as I do, I think about all the different emotions that can cause me to touch this expensive piece of jewellery. Sometimes, it's pride that causes me to handle it, usually when I'm showing it off to a friend or work colleague who compliments me on it and wants to get a closer look. Sometimes, it's happiness that sees me touching it, the feeling of it on my fingers reminding me of the man who loved me enough to give it to me. And sometimes, it's from a place of disbelief that causes me to want to feel it as if I still can't quite believe that I am married and that somebody cares about me more than anybody else in the world.

But today, it's a different feeling that is making me fiddle with the 1-Carat diamond on the fourth finger of my left hand.

It's nerves.

I've noticed myself doing it more and more recently ever since I discovered the lump in my breast while getting ready for bed one night. For some reason, I can't stop playing with my damn wedding ring. Maybe it's because it's a reminder of what I will lose if my diagnosis turns out to be a bad one.

I'll lose the man who gave me this ring.

I'll lose the chance to live a long and happy life full of love.

Realising that fidgeting isn't making me feel any better, I make a conscious decision to let my hands rest in my lap while I focus on the environment around me. This waiting room is clean and clinical, just like every other one I have been in before. The furniture is sparse, just a few chairs lined up in front of a coffee table that is covered in gardening magazines or leaflets on how to talk about mental health. Other than that, there is just a desk opposite me at which a pretty blonde receptionist sits, her manicured fingers tapping the keyboard of her computer as she presumably does whatever a receptionist in a place like this has to do.

She doesn't look nervous like I do, though. Instead, she looks bored, like she is going through the motions simply because it is a means to an end, knowing that when the clock strikes five, she will be out of here and one day closer to payday again. It's hardly an enviable existence, yet I find myself jealous of her. That's because I wish I was bored and simply counting down the hours until I could go and do something more fun. That would be much more pleasurable than how I have felt for the last couple of weeks.

Instead of a life of tedium mixed in with random bursts of spontaneity and excitement, I have been enduring a living hell, consumed by fear and the constant sense of dread that comes when your mortality is put under threat. All I can think about is what if the results of the biopsy reveal that I have cancer?

What will that mean?

Am I going to die and leave my husband as a widow?

As a forty-year-old woman, I can't help but feel like this is unfair. I'm too young to have my life put into doubt. I should be excitedly planning for the next forty years, years which should see me get to accomplish all sorts of wonderful things both in my personal and professional life. I want to continue climbing the ladder in the corporate world, where I am currently holding the position of Finance Manager at a large media marketing company. I want to travel and see all the parts of the planet that I haven't been able to experience yet, including South America, which has always interested me but has remained out of my reach thus far. And I also want to be a mother, getting to give the gift of life and nourishing it, although I'm aware that my biological clock is ticking, and I need to act fast if I want that particular dream to come true.

But it's not the only clock that is ticking.

The seconds might be running out on my time on Earth and all because of a cruel disease that takes no prisoners and usually shows no mercy. There isn't a history of cancer in my family, but that doesn't mean that I couldn't be caught in the crosshairs of the dreaded C-word. Why wouldn't I be? I'm not any more special or unique than anybody else who has ever lived. Millions of people have fallen victim to disease, through no fault of their own. They simply get told by a doctor that they have an illness and there is nothing they can do for them.

Then they fade away into the darkness while life goes on for everybody else.

It isn't fair, but it's the way things are. I've also counted myself as being extremely fortunate, but perhaps this is the time that my luck changes. I got to meet the man of my dreams and marry him, I was able to be in the right place at the right time when promotion opportunities came up at work, and up until a fortnight ago, I had never had anything wrong with my health.

But now I'm about to find out if that has changed.

My appointment with Dr Wilcox is scheduled to commence in five minutes, although I had turned up here early on the off chance that he was running ahead and could have seen me sooner.

That way, I would have been able to learn my fate faster. Alas, it seems I am going to have to wait as long as possible before I get my results.

Before I know it, my fingers are back on my wedding ring, spinning it around my digit and making me a little teary. This item of jewellery is a symbol of the love that a wonderful man has for me, and the only thing worse than the thought of getting bad news today is the thought of having to give it to him later.

My partner's name is Graham, or Gorgeous Graham as a few of my friends jokingly referred to him as, and as well as being good looking, he is an ambitious, hard-working and gentle man who I am lucky to have in my life. But he isn't here with me now, and I'm starting to regret not telling him about this appointment here today. If I had done, I have no doubts that he would have left his office across town and joined me in this waiting room, where he would have held my hand and told me that everything was going to be okay.

I know his presence would have had a calming effect on me, but it was the thought of causing him to worry that has led to me keeping my troubles a secret, for another day at least. So far, Graham has no idea about the lump, nor the fact that I visited the hospital and had a minor procedure to have it examined. I have never kept a single secret from my partner during our four-year relationship, but that streak has been broken now, all because I don't want to make him suffer through all the stress that I have been battling for the last few weeks.

With a bit of luck, my results will be negative, and this will just be my little secret, allowing me to go back to my normal routine and returning to my role as the loving, happy and honest wife. But if not, I am going to have little choice but to break the news to Graham. I'll have to tell him that his healthy wife is now sick. Just like me, he will see his future plans go up in smoke, years of potential parenthood and travelling replaced instead by trips to the hospital and long nights nursing me through my sickness.

I have no doubt that he will support me if it is bad news today. After all, it's what we both signed up for when we took the plunge and got married. We have committed to being there for each other no matter what. It doesn't matter if one of us loses our jobs, or loses our health, or simply loses our way; it is the requirement of the other person to be there to stand by and support them.

With Graham by my side, I often thought I could accomplish anything.

Now, as the door to the doctor's office opens, I hope I was right.

This might be the precursor to the biggest battle of my life.

I might need all the help I can get to survive it.

2

GRAHAM

I pick up the wedding ring from the bedside table and slide it back onto the finger it belongs on as I hear the shower turn on in the bathroom. I think about joining my companion in there but then decide that we've had enough fun for one afternoon, so I remain on the bed instead. It sure is comfortable here, but then I'd expect nothing less in a hotel room that costs £200 a night. The crazy thing is that we're not even staying here for the night. Instead, our total time in this room will amount to a little less than two hours by the time we leave in around thirty minutes. That's because I need to get home to my wife and my acquaintance in the shower needs to get home to her life too.

If it seems rather silly to waste good money on an expensive hotel for such a short space of time, then I'd have to agree, but I don't make the rules. I just do whatever I can to keep this exciting and illicit affair going, and if that means pandering to my partner's request and booking a lavish room for our rendezvous, then so be it. Besides, it's not as if I'm the one who has to pay for it. She covers the costs, and all I'm expected to do is get out of work early and make it to this room with energy and enthusiasm.

So far, I've managed it every time.

As the shower continues to run, I go in search of the remote control for the flatscreen TV that is mounted to the wall opposite the bed in here. It takes me a while to locate it, but I eventually spot it lying on the carpet beside the armchair on which I threw my suit jacket when I arrived earlier. Getting up off the bed, I reach down and scoop up the remote before turning on the TV and returning to my comfortable position, head on the pillow, legs stretched out and not a single thing on my body except the ring I just put back on.

The lady in the shower always makes me take off the ring before we engage in our sordid shenanigans, mainly because she says she doesn't want to be reminded of my wife. That's fair enough, I suppose. But my wedding ring is now safely back on my finger, which is one less thing to worry about. There was a time when I left my ring on the bedside table after one of these secretive hotel liaisons, which caused my wife, Alison, plenty of concern as she thought I'd either removed it on purpose or lost it while at work. In the end, I told her that I had showered at the office after a lunchtime jog and forgotten to put it back on, and she bought it because she knows I always remove my ring before showering.

Speaking of showering, I hear the water in the bathroom suddenly cut out, and I prepare myself for the vision of beauty that is about to enter the bedroom in a few minutes. I can't wait to see Jasmine. That's her name, although it's not really. I don't call her by her real name when we are together, and she doesn't call me by mine. It's just one of the many ways we have made this exciting affair even more exciting. I call her Jasmine, and there's a good reason for that. When we first started this relationship, she asked me what names I found sexy. I struggled to come up with an answer until I remembered that I used to have a crush on Princess Jasmine as a child. Yes, the heroine from Aladdin. Therefore, Jasmine became the name I called her by.

Her name for me is Hugh, and I had assumed at first that she had chosen it because of a crush she had on the famous English actor who had starred in *Love Actually*, amongst many other films. But I was wrong. It was a different Hugh.

She is more of a Wolverine kind of girl.

The nicknames are just one of the many silly games we play to spice things up between ourselves, but I don't need any extra help in feeling all hot and bothered right now. That's because I'm imagining Jasmine entering the room in a moment's time.

I wonder if she will come out of the bathroom with a towel wrapped around her.

I'm hoping not.

As I wait to find out, I entertain myself by scrolling through the channels on the television, skipping past news broadcasts, cookery shows and some awful advertisements before settling on the coverage of the big golf tournament currently underway up in Scotland. I love the sport and hit the fairways as often as I can, but I do also find the game watchable and especially when it's being played in a setting as picturesque as this one. The TV screen is currently filled with a beautiful panoramic shot of the course, and I see the stunning Scottish Highlands as well as the stormy Atlantic Ocean that cuts along them.

It would take a lot to capture my attention from a view like that, but two seconds later and Jasmine manages to achieve it. She steps out of the steamy bathroom wearing nothing but a smile, and despite the beauty on the screen, it pales in comparison to the vision now standing before me.

'Wow,' I say, putting my hands behind my head and taking in the sight.

'How's the golf?' she asks me, glancing at the TV as her wet body shimmers in the light from overhead.

'Screw the golf, come here,' I say, reaching out and pulling her onto the bed, and she doesn't resist, easily falling on top of me and laughing as she goes.

I can feel the edges of her wet hair on the tops of my shoulders, but it's the feeling of her warm bare skin on my own that really makes me come alive, and it's not long until we are kissing again. I figured we were done for the day, but I'm happy to be proven wrong.

But then she lifts up her head, separating her lips from mine, and I wonder if she was just teasing me. That's until she looks down at my left hand and sees that I have put the ring back on.

'You know the rules,' she says, giving me a sly smile.

'Fair enough,' I reply, wasting no time in taking the ring off again and tossing it back onto the bedside table before we pick up where we just left off.

The remote control falls off the bed and clatters on the carpet, but that doesn't make us slow down, nor does the sound of the polite applause from the television where I presume the spectators in attendance are applauding a particularly good golf shot. But then I hear my mobile phone ringing and as much as I want to ignore it like everything else, I can't. That's because the particular ringtone that is sounding now lets me know who is calling.

It's my wife.

'Sorry, one second,' I say, pulling away from the naked woman beside me and reaching for my phone on the table.

'Leave it,' she says as she starts to kiss my neck, and while it is tempting, I know I better not risk it. When Alison calls, I always answer and doing anything differently would only arouse suspicion. That's why I set her number to produce a unique ringtone whenever she phones me, instantly letting me know who it is without having to check the caller I.D.

'Hi. Is everything okay?' I say into the phone while trying to wriggle away from the woman who continues to shower my naked body with kisses.

'Slow down. What do you mean you've been to the doctors?'

Jasmine finally stops kissing me as she realises it might not be the most appropriate time for that now. Not that it was ever appropriate when I'm a married man but never mind.

'Okay, I'll be home as soon as I can,' I say, unsure why Alison is so worked up but figuring it must be something serious for her to be as distressed as this.

I'm just about to hang up when I hear her say the words that I was rather hoping she wouldn't utter. That's because now she has said them, I have to reply in kind, which will be awkward considering my present company.

'I love you too,' I say before ending the call.

'Wow, you know how to make a woman feel good,' my bed buddy says as she moves away from me, getting off the mattress and pulling on the dressing gown that was hanging from a hook on the wall.

'I'm sorry. I've got to go,' I say, getting up myself and going in search of the pair of trousers that I was in such a hurry to rid myself of when I first entered this room not too long ago.

'How is she?'

'I don't know. I think something's wrong.'

'Something's always wrong.'

I ignore that comment and continue getting dressed, pulling on my white shirt before scooping up my tie from behind the armchair, vaguely remembering throwing it there during the fit of passion that had consumed me upon arrival.

'Are you okay if I go?' I ask, not expecting much in the way of disagreement but being polite just in case.

'No problem. You go back to your wife, and I'll stay here and watch the golf.'

I smile at the sarcasm as I head for the door, but before I get there, I take a moment to pull Jasmine towards me and give her another kiss.

‘I’ll see you soon,’ I say, my body wishing we didn’t have to part but my head telling me I need to get going right away.

With that, I leave, exiting the hotel room and rushing away down the corridor in the direction of the lifts. I pass a male cleaner as I go, moving out of the way of his trolley of dirty bed linen, and he gives me the smile of a man who seems to know that I have had a much better afternoon than he has.

While it’s imperative that nobody finds out about my affair, I imagine there isn’t much that a hotel employee doesn’t know when it comes to who is sneaking in and out and what people get up to behind all these closed doors. But that’s okay. This guy can know my secrets.

Just as long as my wife doesn’t.

3

ALISON

I make another check on the street outside my window in the hope that I will see my husband's car pulling onto the drive. But there is still no sign of him, and that means that I'm still unable to share the problem that is currently threatening to overwhelm me and reduce me to a quivering mess.

As I feared, the news from the doctor was not good. The tests revealed that the lump in my breast is malignant, and now I am going to have to undergo surgery before potentially starting what is sure to be several gruelling rounds of chemotherapy. Just like that, all my plans for this year, and indeed the years to follow it went up in smoke.

Never mind thinking about having a baby or even about where to go on holiday this summer; right now, all my energy and focus has to go into giving myself the best chance to survive this. There is no doubt about it; I am fighting for my life, and everything else has to take a backseat to that. But that doesn't mean I have to go through this alone. As well as the support that Dr Wilcox has offered me, I also have my family and friends who I am sure will rally around me once I tell them the sad news. But the person whom I am going to depend on the most over these next few difficult months will undoubtedly be my husband, and he is the first person I am going to break the news to. But a topic this serious means it's best to do it face to face, and unfortunately, I can't do that yet because he isn't home.

I called him half an hour ago and told him I had been to the hospital before asking him if he could come to the house as soon as possible. I knew he would have been at work, but I also know that his job is fairly flexible and the kind of office where people can work from home on occasion instead of being chained to their desk between the hours of 9-5. I also knew he would say yes to my request, one, because I'm sure he could tell how worried I sounded, but two, because he always does whatever I ask him to.

That doesn't mean he is weak-willed or lacks the courage to stand up to me. It's simply because we made an agreement very early on in our relationship that we wouldn't be like all the other couples we knew. They all started off much like us, young and in love, and thinking that nothing could ever go wrong in their perfect relationship. But of course, life has a nasty habit of surprising people, and we saw several of our friends and colleagues go through bitter divorces or stay in unhappy relationships. But we didn't want that, which was why we set some firm ground rules before we entered into legal matrimony.

The first rule is that both of us have to pick up the phone whenever the other person is calling. It doesn't matter where we are or who we are with. What matters is that if one of us wants to speak, the other person listens. I know it might seem a little dramatic that we always have to answer, but I didn't want us to ever get to the stage where either of us considered something else to be more important than answering a call from our partners. Let's face it, nothing in life should be as important as the person you married.

The second rule is that on the eighteenth of every month, we go out for a romantic meal. The reason for that is that number holds great significance in our relationship. Not only was it the eighteenth of the month when we met seven years ago, but it was also the eighteenth when we tied the knot. It's my favourite number and just one more thing that reminds me of my husband, so I make sure that we always celebrate that date on the calendar by forgoing the cooking and putting on our finest clothes before wining and dining each other at an appropriate venue somewhere nice.

And the third rule is a very simple one, and it's one that I imagine most marriages have in place.

No secrets.

Graham and I tell each other everything. Our thoughts, our feelings, our hopes and our fears. Nothing is kept from the other, and that is the way it should be in any healthy relationship. No secrets mean no surprises, and I believe that the fewer surprises there are in a marriage, the better.

So far, there have been none.

Until today.

I have the surprise from hell to give to my husband when he gets home, having to sit him down and tell him about my cancer diagnosis as well as the fact that the prognosis isn't exactly clear yet. I expect that I will burst into tears when I give him the news, and he may even shed a tear or two of his own as well. He is quite an emotional man, and it's just one of the many things I love about him. But I'm rather hoping that he stays strong in this instance, at least when he is around me, because I am going to need all the support I can get. These next few months might be horrendous, and I'm not sure how I'm going to be able to find the strength to get through everything I'm going to have to do.

The operation. The chemo. The array of appointments. And the ability to get out of bed every day and get on with things while battling the nagging thought that it might all be in vain and my days might now be numbered.

Wiping more tears from my eyes, I look outside but still see no sign of Graham. That at least gives me the opportunity to go in search of the box of tissues that I had been looking for when I first got home before giving up and just sobbing into a crumpled-up piece of toilet roll.

I thought I had done enough crying for one day in Dr Wilcox's office when he had given me my test results, but I guess there are still plenty more tears to be shed yet. Fortunately, I find the box of tissues this time, so at least I can be a little more comfortable with all the weeping I still have to do. They were underneath the coffee table again, and I should have looked there first because I know Graham has the bad habit of kicking them under there when he tidies up instead of picking them up and putting them somewhere more useful. That is one of the few habits my husband has that irritates me, but as I think about it now, it only makes me cry more. That's because it's the little things like that which I could soon find myself robbed of if the treatment doesn't work, and I eventually succumb to this horrible disease.

The sound of the car engine outside sends me scurrying over to the window again, and I see the vehicle pulling onto the drive before the door opens and my husband gets out. Graham looks dashing in his suit, as he always does, but the look on his face is one of concern as he hurries towards the front door with his keys in his hand.

I go into the hallway to welcome him home, but it's not going to take much for him to see that things aren't going well. Sure enough, he spots my tear-stained eyes immediately.

'Alison, what's wrong?' he asks as he closes the door and rushes to my side.

I go to speak, but the words catch in my throat, and I just end up hugging him for the first minute he is home.

Graham holds me tightly as I sob into his suit before I eventually pull myself together enough so that I am able to string a sentence together. But just before I utter the dreaded C-word, I notice something is wrong with my husband's appearance.

'Where your ring?' I ask him, noting the lack of jewellery on his left hand.

He instantly looks sheepish, and I'm not surprised because this isn't the first time that he has come home without it on.

'Oh no, I've gone and done it again,' he says, shaking his head. 'It'll be in the shower at work.'

He probably expects me to be annoyed, but I'm not. That's because I have more important things on my mind, so I take him by his ringless hand and lead him onto one of the sofas in the living room before I take a deep breath and give him my news.

4

GRAHAM

It's been ten minutes since my wife told me that she had breast cancer. That means it's been eleven minutes since I realised that I had left my wedding ring in the hotel room where I have spent the afternoon with another woman.

I know I need to get back to the hotel and retrieve the important piece of jewellery before there is an even bigger chance that it gets lost or ends up in the cleaner's pocket, but how can I leave Alison now? She is still crying into my shoulder and telling me how scared she is, so I hardly think that this is the right time for me to tell her that I need to go out again. Instead, I'm going to have to sit here and deal with this situation.

On the plus side, that means I won't be driving anywhere for a while, which would surely be an unwise thing to do given my current state of mind. Of course, I'm shocked at the news that my wife is ill. I had no idea she had developed symptoms of any disease, never mind one as brutal as this. But that's not the only feeling I'm experiencing at this time. I'm also confused, and that's because I'm in love with another woman, meaning that as much as I care about Alison and want her to get better, there is someone I care about even more. And there is one other feeling I have, although it's one that does me no credit.

I'm feeling annoyed.

That's because I was planning on leaving Alison this weekend.

But how am I supposed to do that now when she is like this?

'It's going to be okay,' I tell her, stroking her hair as she continues to weep into my increasingly damp suit.

'How do you know that?' she asks me, and I have no answer for her, mainly because I know that it's not the truth.

While her chances of survival from her illness might be high, the chances of the two of us staying together are not. I know that because I've already given my word to my other woman that I am going to separate from Alison and start a new life with her.

It may not be cancer she has to worry about.

It could be dying of a broken heart.

'I'm sorry,' Alison says, lifting her head up from my shoulder and wiping her eyes.

'Don't be silly. You have nothing to apologise for.'

'I think I need to go and have a lie down.'

'That's a good idea.'

We stand up, and I help guide her towards the stairs before she gives me a kiss and tells me to come and check on her in an hour or so.

I wait until I hear our bedroom door close upstairs before I take my mobile phone out of my pocket and make a call.

'Good afternoon. The Sandalwood Hotel. How can I help you?'

The female voice at the other end of the line belongs to the pleasant woman who greeted me as I walked through the lobby of the hotel earlier today on my way up to the hotel room for my secretive date. She's a pretty receptionist, much nicer than the burly man who sometimes stands there, but right now, I don't care what she looks like. I just need her to help me.

'Hi. I'm sorry to bother you, but I was in one of your rooms this afternoon, number 217, and it seems that I have gone and left my wedding ring on the bedside table.'

'Oh, okay, sir. I hope we can find it for you,' the receptionist says. 'Can I take your name?'

'The room was booked under Jasmine Jackman.'

Yes, she took Hugh's surname as well.

'Is that your wife?'

I pause because not only does the question catch me off guard, but I obviously can't answer it honestly.

'Erm, yeah,' I mumble back, hoping that's all I'll be expected to say on the matter.

I can hear the sound of fingers on a keyboard down the phone before the receptionist speaks again.

'According to this, she hasn't checked out yet. Have you tried calling her?'

On the one hand, it is easier if Jasmine is still in that room because it means a cleaner won't have had a chance to go in yet and either misplace the ring or steal it for themselves. But on the other, I don't really fancy the awkward conversation in which I have to ask my mistress to pick up the ring that is supposed to symbolise my eternal love for my wife.

'Oh, okay,' I say, trying to think on the spot. 'I guess I could try her then. Thank you.'

I hang up, having decided that it wouldn't be worth it to have asked the receptionist if she could have sent somebody up to the room to get it for me. I'll just call Jasmine and ask her to pick it up, however awkward that might be.

Dialling her number, I hold the phone to my ear as I look out of the window onto the quiet street. I'm not often home at this time of the day, so I don't usually get to see all these houses when there are no cars in the driveways or kids playing in the gardens. I'm not sure I like seeing it either. It's eerily quiet out there.

'Missing me already?'

Unlike the last female voice to answer the phone, which was oozing in professionalism, this one is much cheekier and informal.

'Hey. Sorry, are you still in the room?

'Yep. I'm currently lying on the bed snacking on complementary crisps. Why?'

I know it's not going to be pretty, so I just go ahead and get it over with.

'I think I left my ring on the bedside table. Can you check?'

I grimace as I wait for the reaction from the other end of the line, and sure enough, it isn't pretty when it comes.

'Oh yeah, it's here. It was nice of you to leave it for me to look at.'

'Is there any chance you could pick it up, and I could meet you somewhere to get it back?'

'You want me to look after your wedding ring for you even though you know I can't stand the sight of it because it reminds me of her?'

I grit my teeth before answering.

'Yeah. I'm sorry.'

'I've got a better idea,' she says as I watch a delivery van park up outside a neighbour's house and an overweight driver gets out clutching a parcel. 'How about you come back here and get it yourself, and we can have a little fun when you do.'

I roll my eyes as I watch the driver making his way up the driveway, and while I wish I could go back to that hotel room, I know it isn't going to happen. Not when Alison is upstairs in such an emotional state.

'I'd love to,' I say, being honest. 'But I can't. Something's come up at home.'

'You mean with her?'

My silence gives away the answer to that.

'What's happened now?'

I know I'm going to have to tell her about Alison's diagnosis at some point, but I can't handle that conversation at this time. Right now, I just need to get that ring back on my finger as soon as possible and figure out how to proceed from here.

'It's nothing. Just a burst pipe in the kitchen,' I lie. 'I'm waiting for the guy to come out and fix it.'

I hear a deep sigh from the other end of the line, and I'm not sure if I'm going to get my own way until she speaks again.

'I'll meet you on the corner of your street in half an hour.'

Then she hangs up, letting me know just how grumpy she is about having to run an errand involving me and my damn wedding ring.

At least I'm getting it back now. Of course, if everything went to plan, then I would have been losing it for good after this weekend when I intended to end things with Alison and move out. But I'm not sure what I'm going to do now after the shocking news today. There was never going to be a good time to break my wife's heart, but now she has cancer, I'm not sure how I'm going to be able to do it.

I need to think about it.

I also need a strong drink.

5

ALISON

It's been a couple of days since I got the reminder about how fragile life is from Dr Wilcox. Most of that time has been spent feeling sorry for myself, either crying, contemplating or occasionally falling asleep out of sheer exhaustion. I've mainly been asking myself the same questions over and over again.

Will I get better? Will I die? Will Graham be left on his own?

But it's too early for answers yet.

However, it's definitely not too early to get up.

A glance at the time on my mobile phone tells me that it is almost midday, and I should probably think about crawling out of bed. That's because it isn't good to just lie under the duvet and wallow in self-pity for hours on end but also because I have somewhere that I'm supposed to be at two. I had arranged to meet my best friend, Claire, for a coffee on the high street, although those innocent plans were made before I got my bad news. Now, the thought of sitting with my friend and gossiping about silly things like who won the latest series of that reality show we love seems utterly meaningless. But I should go. It will be the best thing for me, or at least it will be before my treatment starts. It will help to do something normal because, let's face it, lying in bed all day and crying is not how I usually spend my weekdays.

I'm fortunate that my employers were sympathetic to my admission that I had cancer, telling me to take as long as I needed and that they were there to support me every step of the way, whether I was able to come into the office or not. That meant a lot and has taken the immediate pressure off me having to put on a brave face and try and carry on as normal. I've told them that I'll be in soon and that I just need some time to come to terms with the diagnosis, and they had no problems with that, which some would take for granted but not me. That's because as a finance manager, it is highly likely that I am going to be missed by the company. But my health comes first right now, as does getting the support of my family and friends.

Fortunately, I've been doing well on that count, and both Graham and my relatives have rallied around me over these last few days. But I still haven't told any of my friends yet about the battle I have ahead of me, though today is the day I change that. I will message several of them on our group chats later and break the news, but first, I want to tell Claire face to face. She is my oldest friend, and I can't tell her something like this over a text message.

We need a good old coffee and a catch-up.

I get out of bed and get dressed before pulling open the curtains and wincing as the bright light hits my vitamin-D deprived skin. I haven't left the house since I got back from my appointment forty-eight hours ago and I've convalesced in this dark bedroom for most of that time since, so the sunlight and the view of my street are not as normal to me as they should be right now.

I go downstairs and put the kettle on, craving a crappy homemade coffee before I get a nicer one at the café with Claire, before tidying up a little around the kitchen as it boils. As usual, Graham wasn't particularly tidy when he made his breakfast this morning before leaving to go to his office, but I'm happy for the distraction as I put his dirty cup and plate into the dishwasher and give the table a wipe down from all the breadcrumbs that he spilt when he was eating his toast.

As I clean, I think about how my husband has handled the devastating news that I ambushed him with earlier. As predicted, he has been a rock of support for me, holding me when I cry, comforting me with words of wisdom as well as making sure to keep me going whenever I needed more tissues or just someone to vent my fears to. But I can also sense the worry he carries within himself now. He is clearly troubled, although he is keeping quiet about everything he is thinking, which I guess is just another one of his ways of making me feel better. Unlike me, he hasn't been verbalising every single thought that has run through his head, no doubt not wanting to make me more worried than I already am. But the fact that I can see how worried he is only makes me more nervous, which is a vicious cycle but one I'm probably going to have to get used to.

But today is not a day for worries. I'm going to be positive from now on and try and seek out the good in this awful situation. While nobody wants to get bad news about their health, one thing it does do is provide clarity of the things that are really important. That means that while normally I would be rushing around in the office at this time of day, asking my colleagues for their reports or signing off a bunch of invoices, I am instead taking my time and appreciating simpler things in life. Like the beautiful view out of my kitchen window as I stand here and wait for the kettle to finish boiling. We really do have a lovely garden, but I don't get to spend half as much time as I would like to in it. But that is going to change now. I'm going to get out in it much more, even if it is a chilly day. I should enjoy the fruits of all my hard work, like this house and the garden, instead of always having my mind on the next deadline at work or the battle of the commute to and from the office.

I'm also appreciative of my husband now, more so than ever. Even though I work hard at my marriage and pride myself on it being as strong as it possibly can, there is no doubt that the events of the last two days have strengthened it even more. Instead of the pair of us being apart for most of the day while we work separately before coming home and running through the banalities of our evening routine, we have sat together for hours and talked, connecting on an even deeper level than I ever thought possible. So as horrible as the news has been, it has made the pair of us even closer than we were before.

I make my cup of coffee and can't wait to drink it, but instead of taking a seat at the kitchen table like I usually would do, I decide that I am going to waste no time in getting into the garden. Unlocking the back door, I step outside and onto the patio, getting my first hit of fresh air in a while. I briefly consider sitting down at the table and chairs we have put out here on the rare occasions we have friends over for a barbecue, but instead, I decide to stay on my feet and potter around, walking over the lawn and getting a closer look at some of the beautiful plants that always start to bloom at this time of year.

But this isn't just any old walk in the garden. I'm savouring everything. The sounds of the birds in the trees. The smell of the freshly cut grass in the neighbour's backyard over the fence. And the sights of all the wonderful examples of life that died out in winter only to be reborn again in spring.

I decide at that moment that I am going to be just like these resilient plants right here. I might have wilted and lost my colour over the last few days as I dealt with the shock of the diagnosis, but that doesn't mean it has to be a permanent state for me now. I can get my colour back eventually, and I can flourish again.

I can be reborn, and who knows; maybe this diagnosis could even end up being the best thing that has ever happened to me.

6

GRAHAM

Why does this always happen to me?

No matter how many plans I make, something always comes along to knock them off track and send me down a different path. It's been a regular theme in my life, and now it has happened again. Alison's cancer diagnosis has come just a few days before I was planning to leave her, when I was going to admit to her that I had fallen out of love and that I wanted the marriage to come to an end. While that would have been a very difficult conversation to have, it would have ultimately freed me up to be with the woman I do want to be with now, and we could have moved away to start the new life we have planned together.

But now this.

Getting up from my desk, I walk over to my office door and close it fully before taking out my phone and preparing to have yet another awkward interaction with Jasmine. It's only been a couple of days since I had to ask her to pick up my wedding ring for me and her mood was decidedly frosty when she handed it to me on my street corner an hour later. But I have a feeling this conversation is going to be even worse than that.

That's because I'm about to tell her that I can't leave Alison yet.

The phone rings four times without an answer, and I start to enjoy the thought that maybe she won't pick up this time and I can delay this uncomfortable situation for another few hours at least. But then I hear the voice at the other end.

Damn. *Jasmine picked up.*

'Hey, it's only me,' I say, trying to keep my voice light before I drop the heavy bomb on her in a moment.

'Hey, you. What are you doing?'

'Just working. The usual.'

'Same. I'm bored. But I can't wait for the weekend.'

I wince because I know exactly what she means. She can't wait because that is supposed to be the time when I turn up at her flat with my bags and tell her that I have left Alison for good. From there, we would have enjoyed cohabiting in her humble abode for a few months while my divorce was processed before going on the lookout for a place we could buy together, somewhere much bigger and somewhere outside of town where I wouldn't have to worry about bumping into Alison while out shopping.

It was such a good plan. It was all set to happen very soon.

And then fate threw a curveball at me out of nowhere.

'Yeah. I need to talk to you about that,' I begin, pacing over the carpet in my office as I try to release some of the nervous energy that is building up inside me.

'Don't even say it,' Jasmine replies, and the sudden change in her tone tells me she has already been anticipating another problem with me leaving my wife.

To be fair, I can't blame her. This wouldn't be the first time I have told her we need to delay things, although all those previous occasions were based on the fact that I was making excuses and still felt too nervous to do it. But now, it's genuinely not about me. It's about Alison. I can't do this to her so soon after the news she has had.

'I'm sorry, but I'm not going to be able to move in with you this weekend.'

I stop pacing and hold my breath. How will she take this?

Then the line goes dead. She hung up on me.

I guess I got my answer.

Shaking my head, I attempt to call her back twice, but the fact that I can't get her to pick up means it's probably best that I just leave it for now, so I do, putting my phone down on my desk and slumping into my office chair.

I knew Jasmine wasn't going to take it well, but I had at least hoped that she would have given me the time to explain my decision. As disappointed as she might be, I'm sure she would have had the compassion to understand why I couldn't leave my wife in the week that she discovered she had a life-threatening illness.

Jasmine might be cold-hearted enough to carry out an affair like I can, but we're not evil. We do still have hearts, and we are still capable of thinking about other people's feelings.

With that in mind, I decide that the best thing for me to do now is to send Jasmine a text message explaining exactly why I just said what I did. I'll tell her about Alison's diagnosis, which will surely garner some sympathy and understanding, before clarifying that I do still intend to leave my wife, just at a more considerate time.

I pick up my phone and type out the message, although the fact that I re-read it and re-type it several times shows how unconfident I am about this working. But after a few minutes of faffing about, I bite the bullet and press send before quickly putting my phone down and not looking at it again like a nervous teenager hoping to get a text back from their crush.

Deciding that it might be a good idea to take my mind off things by getting on with the actual job I'm being paid to sit here and do, I enter my password on my computer screen and get back to work. Life as a data analyst isn't exactly eventful, and as I pore over several spreadsheets that all require me to make sense of an array of numbers, I wonder if my tedious job is one of the reasons why I sought out excitement and risk in my personal life.

Having an affair is many things, including wrong, distasteful and cruel, but it is also adventurous and can lead to all sorts of fun scenarios that brighten up what would otherwise be a fairly dull life. I wonder if I would have sought the thrill of another woman's company if I had been something more exciting or fulfilling like a musician, an author or even a chef. I do like to cook, after all, and a busy kitchen on a Saturday night would certainly be a more stimulating environment than a data analyst's office on a Thursday morning. But maybe it's just yet another one of the many excuses I have given myself to explain why I have broken my wedding vows and betrayed the woman I am supposed to cherish.

Truthfully, I don't think there is just one reason why I cheated. In reality, there are several, and they all contributed in varying degrees, culminating in this mess that I find myself in today. All I can do is accept what I have done in the past and work hard on improving my future. Right now, that means figuring out the best way to keep both Alison and Jasmine happy.

But the unsettling feeling in my stomach warns me that there is another storm brewing on the horizon. It's a problem that I have so far tried to avoid thinking about too much, but one that came to me in the early hours of the morning just after Alison had told me about her diagnosis. The pair of us had been sitting in bed together, tired but unable to sleep, and I was comforting my wife as she progressed through various stages of grief, fear and acceptance. It was then that I realised that I still cared deeply for her and couldn't bear to see her in such a distressed state.

It was also the time I realised that I wasn't entirely convinced that I wanted to leave her.

That thought was a shocking one for me, mainly because I have spent the last few months thinking about nothing but leaving. My affair with Jasmine began over a year ago, and in all that time, I've spent most of it thinking about the new woman in my life instead of the old one. But the reality check from the doctor that Alison might not be around forever has given me pause for thought, and now the idea of not having her in my life at all is an unsettling one.

Do I still love her? On some level, I must do, yes. But is it enough to backtrack on what I have started to build with Jasmine? I don't know.

But one thing is for sure; I better decide soon.

It's hard enough keeping one woman happy, let alone two.

7

ALISON

The café is surprisingly busy for a weekday afternoon as I make my way inside and spot Claire sitting at the table by the toilets. I imagine it's the fact that this place is almost full that has led to her choosing the seats all the way over there because there isn't exactly much choice to sit anywhere else.

I give her a wave as I move around the other tables, dodging baby strollers, super-caffeinated mothers and old people who are frittering away their pensions on over-priced coffees and buns. Finally, I make it to my friend, and I'm about to give her our customary hug when she stops me and frowns.

'Are you okay?'

Maybe it's the bluntness of the question that catches me off guard and causes me to cry. Or maybe it's because I'm slightly overwhelmed by suddenly being in such a busy venue where everybody else here is more concerned with things like sugar, sandwiches or silly gossip while I have death on my mind. Whatever it is, I find myself bursting into tears.

‘Oh my gosh, Alison! What’s wrong?’

I allow my friend to guide me into one of the chairs at our table before picking up a napkin and dabbing at my eyes as if that will somehow cover up the raw emotion that just poured out of me.

‘Oh, Claire, I’m sorry. I’ve just had the worst news.’

Before my emotions can get the better of me again, I quickly run through what has happened recently. The lump. The results. The diagnosis. The uncertainty. I also note the varying degrees of shock on my best friend’s face as she processes it all.

‘I’m so sorry. I had no idea you had even been worried about something like this,’ she says, reaching out and giving my hand a tight squeeze.

‘I hadn’t told anyone until I got my results. Not even Graham.’

Claire looks a little surprised by that admission, so I decide to quickly explain it.

‘I guess I was just hoping that the tests would come back clear, and I wouldn’t have to worry anybody about it.’

‘But we’re here to support you,’ Claire says, still holding my hand and making me feel better already. ‘I wish you’d told me sooner. I feel so foolish now. There I’ve been, texting you about silly things I’ve seen on TV while you’ve been going through this.’

I laugh. Claire has been texting me lots of silly things she has seen on TV recently, although she has been doing it for years. We've been best friends for four years now, ever since we met in the staffroom of the company that I am currently still working at. We bonded as colleagues before rapidly progressing into friends outside of the office, and even when she left for another job, we kept in touch and have continued to see each other almost every week since.

Mid-thirties might seem like a funny time for a woman to make a new best friend, but it wasn't as if I was unpopular before meeting Claire. I did have friends, and I still have many of them now. It was just that I had never met someone whom I connected with before on such a strong level. We didn't just have things in common at the time we met, like a career in finance, loving partners and a thirst for a strong beverage every Friday afternoon when the clock struck five. We also seemed to have a deeper connection when it came to the types of conversations we would have. Nothing has ever been off-limits between us, both good and bad, and we always tell each other everything about our personal lives without shame or the worry of embarrassment. That's why I feel a little guilty now for not letting Claire in on what I have been going through recently. I should have told her sooner, just like I should have told Graham.

A problem shared is a problem halved, as they say. But I've done it now, and I do feel better for it.

I've also stopped crying again, which is a bonus.

Claire has left the table to grab us a couple of coffees and a piece of cake, and I use the time she is away wisely, drying my eyes, blowing my nose and generally pulling myself back together. By the time she returns, I am much more composed and ready to make this as normal a coffee catch-up as possible without it descending into a tsunami of tears again. And I know just the way to do it.

'So, tell me about how you have killed Andy this week,' I say before taking a sip of the lovely coffee that makes my homemade stuff taste like dishwater.

'Two words,' Claire says, a mischievous grin spreading across her pretty face. 'Hedge clippers.'

'Ouch,' I reply, grimacing as I imagine her ex-husband coming face to face with those snapping blades.

'Oh yeah, he really suffered this week. Let's just say I chopped off a lot more than just his fingers.'

I burst out laughing and not just because of the humorous comment. It's also because Claire kept such a straight face as she said it. She really is witty and has a knack for comic timing. She's much funnier than me, as well as better looking, although thankfully, she doesn't acknowledge either of those things or let them dictate the kind of person she is.

'Poor Andy,' I say. 'But I still think that's not as bad as the meat cleaver.'

'Yeah, that was a good one. Maybe I'll use that again next week.'

We both smile at each other before we take another sip of our drinks and look around for the waitress who is supposed to be bringing us our cake. Our jokey discussion about the different ways Claire has murdered her ex-husband, Andy, is all fantasy and just one of the many things we came up with as a way to help her deal with the trauma of the break-up. It was two years ago when Andy left Claire, telling her that he had been unfaithful and that he no longer wished to be tied down by marriage, instead longing to be free and single again despite his advancing years.

To say it came as a shock to the poor woman was an understatement, and I'll never forget the night Claire turned up on my doorstep, bawling her eyes out and asking me if she could come in. We sat up for hours that evening as she talked to me about the breakdown of her marriage and how she had no idea that the man she loved had been betraying her behind her back. Even though we had consumed a bottle of wine during that difficult conversation, it had been a sobering time and one that made me realise how lucky I was to have Graham. I couldn't imagine what it must have felt like to have the man you love stab you in the heart and walk out the door never to return, and I hated the fact that my best friend had to go through that horrible experience. But since then, Claire has slowly but surely regained her confidence, and now we can laugh about her failed marriage and fantasise about all the ways she would kill that foolish ex-husband of hers.

As the waitress finally delivers the cake to our table and I hungrily eye up the sweet treat, I have another reason for feeling optimistic, and it's not just to do with food. It's also because being with Claire and witnessing her progression from devastated wife to flourishing singleton again has shown me that things can get better, and something good can eventually come from something bad. I hope that will be the case with my cancer diagnosis, and I hope that one day I will be able to sit here with my friend and joke about it, jesting about some of the treatment I had or how I used to look when all my hair fell out. It seems impossible to laugh at it now, but it also seemed that way for Claire when she first found out her husband was leaving. Yet here she is, happy again, and it proves to me that I could get to that same place one day soon too.

'Damn, I forgot to bring your coat again,' I say, suddenly remembering the thing I was supposed to do that had completely slipped my mind. Claire left one of her coats at my house a few weeks ago when she called around for wine. She got so drunk she left without it, and it's been sitting in my spare bedroom ever since.

'Don't worry about it. The weather's warming up now, so it's not urgent.'

With that said, we waste little time tucking into the cake, and as we do, I smile to myself because I'm feeling much better now.

I also make a vow to myself to maintain a positive mindset from this point on.

No more thinking about bad luck, scary symptoms or death.

From now on, I'm focusing on all the best things in life.

Family. Friendship. Laughter.

And love.

8

GRAHAM

I've been trying to focus on work all day, but it hasn't worked. That's because I can't stop thinking about the two women in my life. Alison, a woman of great courage, strength and security. And Jasmine, a woman of great desire, passion and unpredictability.

Each of them has qualities that I find attractive and, in some cases, irresistible. But the problem is I can only be with one of them going forward. I have got away with having them both for long enough, but that time has come to an end, and now I have to choose.

My wife or my lover.

Security or unpredictability.

Alison or Jasmine.

But what chance do I have of making a decision like that when I can't even decide what to make for dinner?

I've been standing in the kitchen for the last twenty minutes going between the fridge and the cupboards, trying to figure out what I can cobble together to make a decent meal while Alison rests in bed upstairs. But so far, I have come up with nothing, unless you can count ham pasta, which only a student would do.

Closing the cupboard door again, I realise how out of my depth I truly am. If I can't make a simple decision like this, then how can I decide which woman to upset this weekend?

I know that the clock is ticking on how long I have left to tell Jasmine my intentions. She was clearly annoyed when I spoke to her over the phone earlier today, and she has every right to be. I have promised her the world, and yet here I am, still living with another woman and not committing either way. It's selfish of me to be stringing both of them along like this, although I'm clearly a very selfish person to be able to even get to this point right here. I doubt there are many caring and considerate people who suddenly find themselves having affairs.

My extramarital relationship with Jasmine began at a time when I was having doubts about the decisions I had made in my life up to that point. I was bored at work. I was bored in my social life. And I was bored with the woman I had married. Even though to an outsider I knew it would have looked like I had it all, I couldn't help thinking that I had gone wrong somewhere and made decisions that had led me down a path that only seemed to lead to frustration and a burning desire for more excitement in my life.

Of course, I first tried dealing with those emotions like many people in the same boat do. I used vigorous exercise to lose weight and hopefully make me feel better about myself. I took up new hobbies to hopefully reinvigorate my zest for life. And when those things didn't work, I did the only thing left to do, which was start drinking more and more alcohol. One glass of wine after work turned into two and three, and Friday and Saturday nights were just an abomination of red wine, whiskey and anything else I could find lurking at the back of the kitchen cupboards.

Like alcohol has a tendency to do, it numbed my emotions for a few hours, only to send me down to even worse depths of despair the next day. I knew I had to curtail my drinking even before Alison started to pass comment on it and asked me to cut down.

Like a good husband, I did as I was told, but having exhausted all options I could think of to introduce some excitement back into my life, I was feeling lower than ever.

And then I bumped into the woman who would remind me what it was really like to be alive.

It wasn't the first time I had met Jasmine when we found ourselves sharing the same swimming pool at the local gym that fateful night a year ago. But it was the first time either of us had spoken at any great length to each other without the presence of anybody else around us. It was also the first time I realised I wasn't alone in how I felt about life at that time.

Jasmine was bored too. But unlike me, she had an idea of how to spice things up.

Her suggestion that I come back to hers after the gym came as we had climbed out of the pool and were drying off before heading back into the changing rooms. I thought she was joking at first. I even remember laughing. But then I realised that she was deadly serious and was genuinely giving me the chance to be intimate with her if I wanted to be.

I knew it was wrong. I also knew that I should have just gone into the men's changing room and pretended like it had never happened.

But I didn't.

I felt excited. I felt nervous. I felt alive.

That's why I told her that I would go back to her place.

Those next two hours we spent in each other's company were amongst the best hours of my life and not just because of what we were doing. Rather, it was how our actions made me feel. I felt needed. Wanted. Desired. And I felt like I was a teenager again, rather than a man in his mid-thirties who thought spontaneity and risk were just things of the past.

Of course, I felt guilty when I left her home that night and went back to Alison. Despite my desire for something new, I still loved my wife and wouldn't have wanted her to have ever been hurt. But I also couldn't stop myself, and before long, that one-off with Jasmine had turned into a full-blown affair which has eventually led to the situation we find ourselves in now.

We are in love with each other, and we want to let the world know.

But there is one obstacle to that happening, and it's a huge one. Not only am I still married, but my wife has no idea that I'm cheating on her. Technically, I have gotten away with what I have done so far, but that honeymoon period is over. Now, somebody has to get hurt.

It's just a question of who.

I can't believe that I'm even entertaining the idea of choosing Alison over Jasmine, having spent the longest time certain that I would leave my wife and start afresh with a new relationship. But her diagnosis has sent me into a tailspin, and now I'm confused and not just because I feel sorry for Alison and wish to support her through the next few difficult months. It's also because it has brought into sharp focus just how much I still care about her.

It's only the vibration of my mobile phone in my pocket that snaps me out of my internal debate, and I look at the screen to see who is calling me.

It's Jasmine.

I expect she wants clarification about whether I am ready to leave my wife or not. But I'm not ready to give my answer yet, so I stall on picking up until she eventually quits calling. But any hopes I might have had about a temporary reprieve are quickly dashed when the text message flashes up on my screen a few seconds later.

Either you tell her this weekend, or I do.

I lower my phone, my head spinning and my heart hammering in my chest. Of all the things I have been worried about lately, Jasmine giving me an ultimatum was not one of them. I didn't think she was the kind of person to do such a thing, and it stings me a little that she has done this. I thought she loved me. If so, how could she put me under this much pressure? But then I look at it from her point of view instead of my own. Maybe this proves that she really does love me because she simply can't bear to wait any longer for us to be together properly. She is forcing my hand, not because she hates me but because she wants me so much.

I am just about to reply to the message and ask for more time when I hear Alison calling me from upstairs. It sounds like she wants another drink, so I better get to it, deciding that I'll reply to the message later. But I better not leave it too long.

I've spent all day deliberating over my decision.

But now, it seems like Jasmine is prepared to make it for me.

9

ALISON

My Friday started with a phone call from the hospital to give me the details of my surgery which I'm told is now scheduled for next Thursday. That is soon, much sooner than I had anticipated, but as Graham told me, it's a good thing. The sooner they operate, the sooner they get the tumour out of me, which will stop it from spreading and getting worse.

Unless it already has, and they're already too late.

But that's negative thinking, and I promised myself I wouldn't do that anymore, so I focus on the positive instead.

In less than a week, I will be out of surgery, and that lump will be out of my body. Then I will take things from there, one step at a time, with my husband by my side every step of the way.

Thinking of Graham makes me wish he hadn't had to go into the office today. With his job, he could easily work from home if he wanted to, and he often does, sometimes as much as three times a week on occasion. But he said he had to go in today for some important meeting, so I kissed him goodbye and watched him drive away, wishing that we could have spent the day together but understanding that his job is important, just like mine is.

That's when I get another pang of guilt about the fact that I haven't been into my office since just before I got the diagnosis. I feel bad because it's the end of the month which means it's the busiest time for my finance department, but there is no way I'm in the right headspace at the moment to deal with payment runs and invoice queries. I have told my boss I'll be in on Monday but that I just needed the weekend to finish coming to terms with what is going on with my body these days. He told me that was fine, as well as being okay with the fact that from next Thursday, I'm going to be signed off sick from work for a few days while I recover from surgery. Fortunately, it's only a lumpectomy, meaning the recovery period is much quicker than if it was a more invasive procedure involving the removal of more tissue than just the area causing concern. The fact I only require this type of procedure at this stage is also a good sign that it has been caught early. But I won't know for sure until it's all done and my lymph nodes have been checked.

I shake my head as if to remove the damn C-word from inside my brain before leaving the house and returning to the back garden again, where I have been enjoying the mild weather today while consuming coffee and messaging old friends on my phone. I've acted on my urge to spend more time outdoors now and appreciate nature, as well as finally got around to telling everybody whom I care about what is going on in my life at this moment in time.

My phone has not stopped ringing or receiving messages ever since I started letting my loved ones know my news. The show of support is overwhelming and has caused me to shed a few tears today, although these are purely tears of happiness rather than the horrible kind that gripped me so much earlier in the week. I really am lucky to have so many people who care about me, and it's given me even more strength and determination to fight my illness head-on and emerge from it a healthier and better version of myself.

As I take my seat on the wicker chair that Graham and I picked up from the garden centre last summer, I scroll through my messages to make sure I haven't forgotten to reply to any of the well-wishers who have bombarded me with support today. It seems like I've responded to them all until I notice the unread text from Claire.

Opening it up, I see that she has sent me a meme of a woman in hospital winding up the doctors with her crazy demands. The implication is that this will be me next week when I go into hospital, and I laugh at the joke before replying with several smiley emojis and an assurance that I will do my best to drive everybody on my ward mad with my batty ways.

Putting my phone down, I sit back in the chair and look out over my garden, admiring the grass that Graham has promised to cut this weekend, as well as the flowerbeds that need a little revitalising but are still much neater than anything my neighbours have in their gardens judging by what I have been able to see of them from the upstairs window.

This is quite the home to be proud of, and it's taken a long time to get it how Graham and I dreamt of, but now we have, and as the saying goes, hard work pays off. We've worked hard in our careers to earn good money, we've worked hard to make this house as comfortable for us as possible, and we have worked hard to make sure that our relationship is rock solid and able to survive anything that comes our way. With that in mind, I am confident that there is nothing on the horizon that we can't deal with.

Little did I know it at that time, but I was wrong.

In reality, that moment in the garden was one of the last times I would be happy before my entire world imploded and sent me off down a path that would not only shock those who knew me but every single person in this town.

10

GRAHAM

Yet again, I've told another lie to my wife. This time it was about the existence of an important meeting that has required me to attend the office today instead of working from home as planned. There is no meeting, and I'm not in the office right now. Instead, I'm standing on the high street waiting to meet Jasmine so I can hopefully talk her out of doing what she has threatened to do this weekend, which is blow up my marriage.

Checking my watch again, I see that she is five minutes late, and I'm not sure if I should read anything into that. It may be that she has been delayed in leaving her workplace and getting down here, which would be perfectly understandable considering this is the middle of a working day. But on the other hand, it may be because she isn't going to turn up, making good on her message in which she said that she might not show up at all because she was so fed up with all the messing about between us.

I sincerely hope it is the former and not the latter because if not, then I am definitely in trouble, and Jasmine is serious about her intentions to tell Alison what has been going on. But then I catch a glimpse of blonde hair further up the street and see that the woman walking towards me now is the woman I have arranged to meet.

Making sure to put a smile on my face to disguise how stressed I really am on the inside, I greet Jasmine and hope to receive a similarly warm welcome in return. But no such luck. Jasmine is wearing that frown of hers that I usually find so sexy, only this time it just looks plain terrifying.

'What do you want?' she asks me as several pedestrians scurry around us on the busy street carrying shopping bags and pastry packets from the local pie shop that always does a good trade.

'Don't be likc this.'

'Like what? I think I have a right to be annoyed considering you have been lying to me.'

'I haven't lied to you.'

'You told me you would leave Alison this weekend, and now you are backtracking again. How is that not lying? You can lie to your wife all you want, but you never lie to me.'

'I know that, and I know I said I would do it this weekend. But that was before I found out she had cancer.'

I hope the mention of the C-word will elicit some sympathy from Jasmine, but no such luck.

'It's terrible if she is ill but let's face it, you haven't been husband of the year, have you? So why do you suddenly care about her now?'

'There's a big difference between leaving a healthy woman and leaving one that is ill and needs all the support she can get.'

'So what? Are you staying with her now? Is that it?'

I pause before answering, mainly because both of our voices have been getting increasingly louder since this conversation began, and I don't want anybody overhearing what we are talking about. If it had been up to me, I would have had this meeting somewhere a lot quieter, but it hadn't been. Jasmine had set the time and place, and it was this busy street or nothing.

'Look, I just don't want to do anything that is going to make Alison feel worse than she already does at this time. Maybe when she recovers, it will be a better time to have that conversation. But right now, she has a huge battle on her hands, and me breaking her heart isn't going to help that.'

'I knew it. You were never going to leave her. You were just stringing me along so you could have the best of both worlds.'

'No, that's not what I was doing at all.'

'Isn't it? Then how come every time it gets to the moment when you promise me you will leave her, something comes up.'

She is referring to the last time I promised her that I would leave my wife. It was last month when I was just about to say the words to Alison when she got a phone call to find out that her grandmother had passed away. That surprising call had forced me to backtrack on my plans and refrain from leaving Alison until a later date. But now that later date is here, and I am trying to delay it again.

'You have to admit it would be a pretty shitty thing to do to leave my wife in the same week that she found out she had cancer,' I say, expecting that to at least get me some form of agreement. But once again, I'm wrong.

'It's always going to be a bad time, whenever you do it,' Jasmine replies, shaking her head. 'You've been cheating on your wife. There isn't a good time to tell her that!'

I grimace as Jasmine's loud voice cuts through the background noise of the high street, and I notice an elderly man with a walking stick stop and look in our direction, presumably interested in hearing a bit more gossip that he can tell the rest of the old boys down the local pub about tonight. But I deny him the chance, taking Jasmine by the arm and leading her down the side of one of the shops to where fewer people can overhear the rest of our conversation.

'Just give me a few more weeks. That should be enough time to find out if the cancer has spread or not.'

'And what if it has?'

The thought of that is terrifying for me, but I don't let Jasmine see that. I can't let her know the full extent of how much I am worried about my wife because then she would quite rightly assume that I'm still not entirely sure if I want to leave her.

'I don't know. I guess I'll just have to assess it then.'

'No, this isn't good enough,' Jasmine says, pulling her arm away from me. 'Either you tell her tonight, or I tell her tomorrow.'

'I can't do that.'

'Then I'll do it for you.'

Jasmine turns to storm away, but I grab her arm again and pull her back towards me, desperate because I have no doubt that she is serious.

'Please. It'll destroy her if she hears it from you.'

'I don't care as long as she hears it from someone. I can't put my life on hold any longer.'

'What do you mean by that?'

'I mean that I'm not going to wait forever for you. If you can't leave your wife, then I will find myself a man who really wants to be with me.'

'Don't be ridiculous!'

‘I’m not. I’ve had enough of waiting around for you to leave her. I feel like you don’t even want to do it.’

‘Maybe I don’t.’

The words are out of my mouth before I have the chance to catch myself, and I regret them instantly, but it’s too late for that now, and Jasmine glares at me like she has every right to.

‘You’re not serious?’ she asks me.

I realise I’ve been honest up to this point, so I might as well continue with that tactic and see where it gets me.

‘Maybe I am. Yes, we’re good together, and yes, I was willing to leave Alison for you, but I’ve seen a different side to you today, and I’m not sure I like it.’

That is mostly true. Hearing Jasmine be so uncaring with regards to Alison’s illness has definitely put me off her, as well as the fact that she had the nerve to give me a ridiculous ultimatum, as if my marriage was some kind of 50/50 choice on a TV gameshow. But it’s also because I have felt my feelings for my wife reignite this week since her life has come under threat, and I’m curious as to what that might mean for our relationship going forward. Maybe it’s not my marriage that has run its course but my affair instead. It has been fun, and it has reinvigorated me, but perhaps everything I ever needed is already waiting for me at home.

'If you stay with Alison, then we are finished,' Jasmine tells me, stating the obvious but putting it out there anyway.

She is defiant, so I feel like being the same with her.

'Then I guess we are finished,' I say, trying to remain calm as I utter the words that I know are going to be a dagger through Jasmine's heart. But better hers than my sick wife's.

She looks at me, shocked and saddened and almost unsure what to do with herself before she turns and walks away. I think about calling after her, but I decide not to. She needs time to think, and so do I. But at least I have dealt with the problem now. She gave me a choice, and I made it.

My affair is over.

Now it's time to put all my energy back into my marriage.

11

ALISON

It's been a lovely afternoon in the garden, but it's started to get chilly now, and I've had enough fresh air for one day. Now I just want my husband to come home so we can have a nice meal together and take our minds off this hectic week with a good movie. He should be back any minute, and I can't wait. In preparation, I have decided to do something I haven't done for a long time.

I am going to have a go at seducing him.

It seems silly to think that I have to seduce the man I married, and I know I don't have to, really. He'd be happy enough to come straight to bed if I just asked him outright, and there's certainly no need for a silky nightdress or fluttering of my eyelashes. But I'm going to make the effort anyway just because it's nice. He's worked hard all day, and he has worked hard all week in picking me up when I was down and helping me get back into a more positive mindset.

Now it's time for his reward.

Walking into my bedroom, I open the wardrobe and peruse my clothing options inside.

Everything on the hanger is either work-suitable attire or dresses that I haven't been able to fit into for a long time, so there's nothing sexy to be found there. A quick check on a couple of the pull-out drawers at the bottom of the wardrobe also bears little fruit, unless I think that Graham might be turned on to see me wearing a pair of jogging bottoms and some fluffy Christmas socks, which I'm sure he won't be.

Heading over to my dresser table, I open the top drawer to see if I buried anything remotely saucy in here a long time ago. It turns out that I have, and I quickly pull out the red lace nightdress that I had forgotten I'd bought before holding it up against myself and trying to figure out if it will still fit me. It's hard to tell without putting it on, so I get to work quickly, aware that Graham could walk through the front door at any second and catch me before I've had a chance to be fully ready for him.

Slipping out of my dowdy clothes and into the seductive nightdress, I run my hands along the smooth material and check my reflection in the mirror to make sure that everything looks okay. To my delight, it looks good on me, although not quite as good as the day I tried it on in the shop where I purchased it. Then again, that was a couple of years ago, and a lot has happened since then, including several trips to the local cake shop.

Happy with how I'm looking fashion-wise, I decide to try and do something about my hair and face, which are just some of the many things that I have neglected during this difficult week. Picking up a comb, I run it through my dark locks although, rather predictably, it catches on several knots, a consequence of not giving it any treatment for the last few days as well as all the time I spent lying on it while I've been in bed. But I'm gradually able to get the comb through my hair until it is looking and feeling much better before turning my attention to the pale and blotchy skin on my face. Even an afternoon in the early spring sunshine has not been enough to put some colour in my cheeks, but it's nothing that a bit of foundation and bronzer can't rectify. With my skin looking much healthier, I get to work on bringing my eyes to life, applying mascara to my long eyelashes, which I intend to use to my advantage when Graham does eventually walk through the door and see what I have in mind for him.

With my work in the bedroom complete, at least for now anyway, I head back downstairs and go in search of a nice bottle of red wine that will help get us in the mood even more when the time comes. Running my fingers along the edges of the six bottles that are currently sitting in the wine rack, I opt for an Australian Shiraz, this one produced in the Victoria countryside just outside Melbourne, which was one of the cities Graham and I were lucky enough to visit on our trip Down Under two years ago. Ever since we got back from there, we have been in love with Aussie wines and make sure to maintain a healthy stock of them via the online retailer we use.

I deliberate on holding off on opening the bottle until Graham walks through the door but decide to have it ready and waiting for him so as not to waste any time. The corkscrew does its job efficiently, and I pour two healthy measures of wine before picking up my own glass and taking a refreshing sip.

I'm not the connoisseur that my husband is, but I do appreciate it much more than the average drinker and am able to detect several different tastes as the fine liquid slips down my throat. But drinking alone isn't much fun, so I make another check on the time and wonder what could be keeping Graham. He told me his meeting was due to finish at four and that he would be home straight after it, but it's now almost five, and there is still no sign of him. If I have to guess, I'd say that it has either overran or he has got caught up chatting with one of his colleagues and has been too polite to end the conversation early and tell them that he has to get home to his wife.

That's my husband. Polite, professional and patient.

Unlike me. I'm impatient and growing more impatient by the minute.

Another swig of wine helps take the edge off recent events, and the more I drink, the better I feel not just about the operation next week but also what I have in store for tonight. I'm going to give my husband quite the show because who knows when I'm next going to have the energy again? Depending on the results of the surgery and the type of treatment I require, I could be wiped out for months with gruelling chemo sessions and all the consequences that come from that. I doubt I'll be feeling sexy if I end up needing a wig or even just a hand getting in and out of bed every night. But for the time being, I am fit and full of energy, and I intend to take advantage of that.

I also intend to take full advantage of 'Gorgeous Graham.'

Finally, I hear the sounds of a car engine on the driveway and take the opportunity to top up my wine glass before the front door opens and Graham realises that I started without him. But to my surprise, instead of hearing the sound of his keys in the door, I hear three sharp knocks on it.

Why is Graham knocking? Has he lost his house key?

I guess so because why else would he need me to let him in?

Putting my glass down before walking into the hallway, I make a final check on my appearance in the mirror before reaching for the door handle and pulling it open.

That's when I see the person standing on my doorstep isn't my husband.

It's my best friend instead.

'Claire!' I say, my shocked response almost matching the shocked look on her face.

I didn't expect to see her, and she probably didn't expect to see me half-naked.

'Sorry, is this a bad time?' she asks, and I laugh, but for some reason, she doesn't display the cheeky smile that she usually shows just after she has made a joke. Instead, she looks quite annoyed.

'No, not at all. I was expecting Graham, that's all.'

'I can see that.'

It's another sarcastic joke, but again, she isn't smiling when she says it.

'Is everything okay?' I ask, closing the door slightly so that only my head is on show to the woman on my doorstep.

'No, it's not actually,' she replies, shaking her head. 'I'm here to tell you that I have been sleeping with Graham for over a year now, and this weekend was supposed to be when he finally left you and started a new life with me. But he's chosen you instead. Congratulations. And good luck with that chemo.'

With that, Claire turns and walks away down the driveway, leaving me speechless.

I'm just about to call out to her before she can get into her car when I see Graham arriving back, his own vehicle slowing down as he realises that Claire is blocking his way.

But Claire is in no mood to hang around and quickly speeds off, giving Graham space to now park on the drive. But funnily enough, it doesn't seem like he wants to do that, and he just sits behind his steering wheel, staring through the windscreen at me.

I guess he has figured out what Claire has just told me.

I guess he knows now that he has been rumbled.

12

GRAHAM

The look on my wife's face says it all. I can see it as plain as day as I sit here in my car, avoiding parking up on the driveway and getting out.

She knows everything.

My secrets have been shared, and now my marriage is ruined.

I know I should leave my vehicle and rush towards Alison, telling her that I can explain and that it doesn't have to mean the end of our relationship. But there is another part of me that just wants to stay in the safety of this car, where I am shielded from all the pain, anger and brutal reality of what my actions have resulted in. I even consider putting my foot back on the accelerator pedal and driving off, as if I can just make my escape and leave all of this chaos behind. But I can't do that.

As selfish as I have been, that would be an all-time low.

Instead, I do the honourable thing and park up on the driveway before turning the engine off and opening my door. I can see Alison is still watching me from the doorway, a blank expression on her face like she is either in shock or is being extremely patient and waiting for me to get nearer before she explodes.

There is no doubt this is the last bit of calm before the storm.

'Alison. Listen, I-'

Those three words are all I manage to get out before she slams the front door.

I take a deep breath before entering the house, partly because I need to try and stay calm if I'm going to have any chance of talking my way out of this but mainly because I'm petrified.

I can't believe Jasmine did this, or to use her real name now because our affair is definitely over:

Claire.

Not only did I believe that she wouldn't do this to me, I honestly did not think that she would have it in her to stand in front of her best friend and admit what had been going on. Alison and Claire have been close for four years and meet up almost every week for long chats over coffee and cake, but just like my marriage, that relationship has now imploded too.

It's a double betrayal for Alison, her husband and her best friend, the two people she would have trusted more than anybody else, and I can't even imagine how she is feeling inside. It kills me that she will be so upset now and will never trust me again. And it kills me that Claire has gotten away with being the one to ruin everything.

I knew as soon as I saw her car parked outside my house that she was here to blow the lid off the affair. After our disagreement on the high street earlier today, I saw no other reason why she would have been around at my house so soon afterwards unless it was to spill the beans and reveal the kind of man I really am. I guess I shouldn't have been so honest with Claire and told her that I was choosing to stay with Alison instead. I obviously broke her heart, and she wanted revenge.

Now she has got it by breaking Alison's.

Putting my key in the door, I hesitate one last time before turning it and going inside, preparing myself for the emotional barrage that is about to come my way.

Will there be tears, or will there be screaming? Will I get a chance to try and get close to my wife, or will I be too busy ducking out of the way of all the things she is throwing at me?

It's too early to tell yet because as I stand in the hallway, I can't see Alison anywhere.

'Alison? Where are you?'

I hear nothing, and the silence is excruciating.

Closing the front door behind me, I battle the sickly feeling in my stomach and push on into the house, looking for my wife in the living room, dining room and kitchen. But she isn't in any of those rooms.

Figuring she must be in the bedroom, I head upstairs, calling out again to her as I go. But to my surprise, the bedroom is also empty, as is the bathroom and the spare room.

Where the hell is she?

'Alison!'

I call out her name, concerned but no longer just for my own safety. I'm worried about hers.

I'm worried that she might have done something stupid.

I'm just about to leave the spare bedroom and head downstairs when I take a look out of the window, and that's when I see her. She is lying on her back on the grass in the back garden, completely still, with her eyes closed.

What has she done to herself?

I race down the stairs and into the kitchen, pulling the back door open and running across the patio towards the body on the lawn.

'Alison!' I call out, hoping that my arrival will be enough to stir her from whatever state of unconsciousness she must have fallen into. But she doesn't move, and as I finally reach her, I brace myself for the first look at any possible injuries she may have inflicted upon herself in her state of distress.

But I see nothing. No blood. No cuts on her wrists or any item lying on the grass beside her that she might have been able to use to cause herself harm.

So why isn't she moving? And why are her eyes closed?

'Alison,' I say, shaking her shoulder and hoping that will get a response from her. If not, I wonder if she has taken some pills and knocked herself out. If so, she needs to be taken to a hospital now.

But then she opens her eyes, and I see that she is alright. She is more than alright, in fact. She is smiling.

And now she is laughing.

'What are you doing?' I ask her, assuming she must be in shock if this is her reaction to the news that I was cheating on her with her best friend.

'I'm just lying on the grass. Why don't you join me?' she replies as if this is a perfectly normal thing to ask.

'Come on. Let me help you up,' I say, trying to get my hands underneath her body so I can lift her off the ground, but she pushes me away and sinks down deeper into the grass.

'I want to stay here. I like it here.'

She looks like she means it and the smile on her face remains. But this doesn't make any sense. She should be shouting and screaming at me, as well as telling me to pack my bags and get out of the house. But she isn't doing any of those things, and while I'm grateful for that, I'm unnerved by this unpredictability.

Grief and anger I can deal with. But this is just weird.

'Alison. I'm sorry,' I say, sitting down beside her when it's clear that she isn't going to get up. 'You have to give me a chance to explain.'

'I don't want to know,' she tells me, shaking her head as she stares up at the sky.

'Do you hate me?' I ask. 'You must hate me?'

'No, I don't hate you.'

The response is unexpected but a good one. Maybe I have a chance of salvaging this. But then she speaks again.

'I don't hate you. I despise you with every fibre of my being. I find you repulsive, just like her. And I want you to get in your car and drive away from here, just like she just did.'

'Alison, wait-'

'If you don't go now, then I am going to stab you to death with a kitchen knife,' she goes on, her calm voice and stoic expression not at all in sync with the aggressive and downright frightening thing she has just told me.

'Don't be silly,' I say, but then she turns to look at me, and I see that she isn't. There is a burning rage behind her eyes that lets me know that she is deadly serious.

'I'll get some things and stay in a hotel tonight,' I suggest, getting to my feet quickly. 'But give me a call when you want to talk. Please, Alison. You have to give me the chance to talk to you.'

Alison closes her eyes again, effectively signalling that this conversation is over, at least for now anyway, so I reluctantly head back towards the house.

I meant what I said about packing a few things and checking myself into a hotel tonight. But I also meant what I said about the fact that my wife and I need to talk. There is no way I am giving up on this marriage without a fight.

But as I head up the staircase on my way to pack my bags, I am firm in my belief about something else too.

There is also no way I am going to let Claire get away with what she has just done.

13

ALISON

I'm not sure how long I was lying on that grass for in total, but I do know that the sky had turned from grey to black, and the temperature had dropped an awful lot by the time I did get up and go back inside. When I did walk in and close the door, the house was silent, as it should have been in the absence of my husband who I had told to leave before I harmed him.

He said he is going to go to a hotel, so I presume that's where he is now, but I could be wrong. He could have been lying to me, as he so clearly has been doing for a while. He might not be at a hotel, and he might not be alone.

He could be with her.

Claire did not look like my best friend when she stood on my doorstep earlier and told me that she had been having an affair with my husband. There had been a coldness to her, and it was that coldness that told me she was telling the truth. That's why I didn't ask her for any more details before she walked away up the drive and got back into her car, and it was also why I didn't question

Graham when he walked in a few moments later. Instead, I just went and lay down on the grass in the garden, which would have made little sense to my husband when he came out and found me there, but I felt he deserved to feel confused. That's because I was confused too.

I was confused as to how I could have ever thought that either of those people were worthy of my affection.

Claire's betrayal is in breach of an unwritten rule, which is that you do not sleep with your friend's partner. But Graham's is so much worse, shattering the vows that we both said to each other in that church before making a mockery of the certificate that we signed which was supposed to prove to the world just how much we loved each other.

I've lost two people who were close to me in one day, but I've also lost so much more. I've lost my identity as a wife and as someone who is capable of being loved by another man.

What does this leave me as?

A sick, unlovable loser?

I don't want to know the answer to that, so I ignore it and instead try to figure out where I am going to go from here. I have a lot of uncertainty ahead of me in regard to both my illness and now my personal relationships. But there is one thing I am already certain on, and I doubt my conviction for it is going to waver anytime in the near future.

I am certain that I am going to get revenge.

Graham and Claire are going to pay for what they did to me. They deserve to, and they will. But what form my revenge will take has not come to me yet. I'll have to sleep on it, and sleep on it I will. I'm sure that by the time I wake up tomorrow morning, a plan will have formed in my mind, and it will be one that will result in the demise of my husband and my best friend.

I'm not overreacting now or having my judgement clouded by emotion. That's not what is happening here at all. What is happening is that I know exactly what needs to be done, and that is total and absolute revenge on the two people who have stabbed me in both the back and the heart. I look forward to seeing both of their faces when they realise that their biggest mistake wasn't in betraying me but rather in their belief that they could get away with it.

I'm not sure why Claire decided to tell me about the affair, but one thing is clear. She thinks there will be no consequences for her other than the end of our friendship. She obviously expects Graham to bear the brunt of my anger and retribution and probably believes her involvement in my life is now at an end. But she couldn't be more wrong.

She has no idea who she has messed with and what is coming to her.

As for my husband, I'm sure his head is filled with all sorts of worries that revolve around things like divorce or the fear of being alone. He will be afraid that his one night in a hotel will turn into many more as he is forced to move out of our marital home and set up a new life for himself at an age when he probably thought he was settled down. He'll also be wondering if divorce proceedings are on the horizon and how much that is going to cost him, no doubt fearful of lawyers swooping in and making him give up half of everything he has worked hard to accumulate over the years. But just like Claire, he has no idea what he should be really worried about. Divorce would be a walk in the park for him if I was to take him down that path, at least compared to what I really want to do to him, which is destroy him in every single possible way. By the time I'm done with him, he'll be begging to give me everything he has just so I stop.

But I won't listen.

I'll never listen to that man again.

The challenge I have now isn't mending my broken heart or even staring cancer in the face and beating it. It is making Graham and Claire think that I am reacting to the news of their betrayal in a normal way. They will be expecting anger, and frustration and shock, as well as many questions to find the truth. In all honesty, I don't care much for the truth anymore after what they have done, but they will think that I do, so I better behave accordingly. I need them to think that all of this mess will die down and that while our relationships are ruined, life will go on.

But it won't go on. Not for them and maybe not even for me, depending on what the doctors tell me over the coming few weeks and months. But that's okay. Maybe it doesn't have to be a bad thing.

In a world this screwed up, who wants to live forever anyway?

I thought I did. I've spent the last few days worrying about death and being scared to meet my maker. But not anymore. Not after what just happened.

Now all I give a damn about is making the most of being alive. Those two liars have given me a new hunger, and it's one I haven't felt in a long time. But maybe it's just what I need after spending so long coasting through life in the slow lane. I used to be determined, ambitious, and most of all, the kind of person whom nobody would ever dare treat in such a disgusting way. But I guess I lost that somewhere over the years and became an easy target.

Predictable. Pathetic. The kind of woman who husbands cheat on and friends laugh about behind their backs.

Maybe that's why I'm sick now.

Maybe I've completely lost the essence of what made me who I am.

But I'm back now. I can feel it in my bones as I stand here in this empty house and stare at the photographs on the mantelpiece of Graham and I on our wedding day. I could be forgiven for those photos making me angry or upset, but they don't.

They just make me feel motivated to get my own back.

What I really need is a photo of Graham and Claire together. There must be one of them around here somewhere. Lord knows they have attended enough of the same parties over the years alongside me.

I need to find such a photo, and I need to keep it close so that I can look at it every day.

That way, I won't ever feel bad about what I am going to do to them.

14

GRAHAM

'Another beer?'

The question is an obvious one for a barman to ask and the answer I give him is no less surprising.

'Yeah, go on then.'

As I watch the uniformed hotel employee pick up an empty pint glass and put it underneath the beer tap, I wonder just how many more I should allow myself before I finally decide to call it a night. This next one will be four, and that's probably pushing it for a weeknight. But this isn't just any old weeknight.

This is the night before my wife goes in for surgery, and I am not able to be with her to provide support.

Of course, that is my own fault, and I'm not looking for sympathy from anyone, not even this barman as he serves me the fresh glass of frothy liquid. But what I am looking for is a way to make my wife forgive me for what I have done and allow me back into our home so I can not only start trying to make amends with her but also provide her with all the help she needs to get through her cancer treatment.

It's been almost a week since Claire dropped the bombshell on my doorstep and walked away, leaving behind a shattered marriage and sending me into this dreary life of living out of a suitcase in this crappy hotel. In that time, I have begged Alison to take me back, or if not, then at least give me the chance to explain myself and make her see that while I have been foolish and despicable, I still love her and want to make our marriage work. But so far, she has remained resolute in not giving me that opportunity and has only allowed me back into our home to get more clothes, which has been helpful but is still a long way from what I really need to make happen.

The last time I was at the house, I asked her how long she was going to make me stay in this hotel until she came to a decision on what she was going to do about my affair. But she just said she needed time and that she wanted me out of the way so she could focus on beating her illness. While that was frustrating, I do realise the importance of her needing to put all her energy into beating her cancer, so I have complied with her wishes and been living in this poxy place for several days now. But I just wish I could make her see that my presence at home doesn't have to be a hindrance in her recovery.

Instead, it could be a help.

Honestly, I suppose I should be thankful that she hasn't already mentioned the 'D' word to me. So far, divorce hasn't been brought up, and I'm hoping it never will be. That has to mean something, I guess. Hopefully, it means that she isn't considering it and just needs time to get her head around the shock of what happened. If that's the case, then I'll give her all the time she needs, even if it means having to drink more of this overpriced beer in this overpriced hotel.

Anything to keep my marriage together.

It's funny how it wasn't so long ago that I actively wanted my marriage to be over and was willing to leave it all behind for Claire. Sitting here now, it seems like madness that I ever considered that to be the best thing for me. I guess I really was caught up in how exciting the affair was. But the reality of the situation is that nothing can ever compare to what I had with my wife, and it's just a shame it took me this long to figure that out. If only I hadn't taken her for granted, and if only I hadn't jumped at the first chance to have a little fun on the side, then I definitely would not be sitting here now. I'd be at home, where I belong, helping my wife pack for the hospital and telling her that everything is going to be okay tomorrow.

I pick up my mobile phone that has been sitting beside me on the bar ever since I came in after another day in the office and think again about giving Alison another call. But I know she will just ignore them like she has ignored all my others. She only communicates with me through text messages now, and we haven't spoken face to face in forty-eight hours. That occasion was when Alison asked me to give her more details about my affair, mainly how it had started, how long it had been going on and how it had ended with Claire standing at the front door spilling our secret. I was glad of the opportunity to converse, even if it was about a topic that was so difficult for me, so I answered every question as honestly as I could, leaving nothing out and giving Alison all the details to work with so that she could come to her decision about what to do next.

But that decision still alludes her and therefore, me.

But it's not just my wife who I have spoken to about the affair in all that time.

I have had words with Claire too.

I wanted to know why she did what she did and how she could possibly have thought that it was the best thing to do for either of us. I expected her to feel some level of regret based on the fact that in her haste to get back at me, she had not only ruined any final chance that I might have chosen her over my wife but also ruined her best friendship too. But she wasn't repentant. She was pleased. In her warped world, she figured that if she couldn't have me, then Alison couldn't have me either. She knew exactly what she was doing when she told my wife about our secret and fully expected Alison to kick me out and never let me back. What she didn't expect was that I believe there is still hope that my marriage can be salvaged.

But for now, I have nothing. No wife. No lover. No one at all to keep me company other than this damn bartender and his horrible uniform. He's looking at me again as I drain another beer, no doubt wondering if I want another one. But I don't. I'm done for the night, and I make that clear by getting up from my stool and gathering up my belongings.

It's the first time I've stood up since I sat down, and I'm much more unsteady on my feet than I was when I arrived, but the alcohol has taken the edge off my bad mood and should help me fall asleep much quicker when my head finally hits the pillow.

As I walk out of the bar that is filled with lonely businessmen, all presumably in town just for one night, I hope that it won't be long until I am making my way back to my own bed and not the crappy one I am basically renting upstairs in this place. I wonder how long it will be until I can lie beside my wife and listen to her breathing as she falls asleep. And I wonder how long it will be until I get to hold her in my arms again and tell her that I love her.

One thing is for sure; if I do get that chance, then I am going to make the most of it.

I'm never going to hurt my wife again.

I'm going to spend the rest of our lives making things right.

15

ALISON

How long do you think the rest of your life will be? Years, surely. Multiple decades if you are lucky. I always used to think the same thing. I thought I had forever. The cancer diagnosis reminded me that I shouldn't take that for granted, but I still liked to believe that I would recover and get over it. But I guess I was wrong.

The doctor has just told me so.

'Six months?' I ask him, repeating back the two words he has just said to me as I sit here in his office and look at the sorry expression on his face.

'Maybe twelve. We'll do everything we can with the treatment options available to us.'

I'm not sure if the potential of an extra six months is supposed to make me feel any better, but if so, it hasn't worked. I thought I had years, plural. But it seems the best-case scenario is a single year. Not only is that way less time than I thought, but it also means everything I wanted to do in my life now has to be condensed into the next few months, and even so, I'll never be able to get through all of it.

Travel. Charity work.

Revenge.

My desire to punish Graham and Claire for what they have done to me has not diminished, but I am going to have to act on it sooner rather than later if I want them to get their comeuppance. That's because my cancer has spread. It's not just in my breast; *it's everywhere.*

The surgery removed the lump, but the check on my lymph nodes showed that it was too late to catch it all. What I had hoped was going to be a gruelling few months of treatment before returning to a long life of health and wellness has suddenly been condensed down into a very short life filled with that same gruelling treatment only this time it won't make one bit of difference. Dr Wilcox has just said as much.

He can only prolong my life, not save it.

I'm screwed. Betrayed by my body. Staring death in the face.

And worst of all, I don't even have my husband or my best friend to turn to.

'I understand that this is very upsetting. Is there anybody that you would like me to call?' Dr Wilcox asks, probably expecting me to give Graham's name.

But I don't. I just shake my head.

'Are you sure? My receptionist can give them a ring right now. It's no problem.'

'No!' I snap back, and the man opposite me flinches a little, clearly surprised by my sudden burst of emotion.

I think about apologising but then realise that I have nothing to be sorry for. I didn't ask for this deadly disease, just like I didn't ask for two people I trusted to embark on a sordid affair together. So why should I say sorry to anyone for anything?

Saying nothing at all, I get up from my chair and head for the door, ignoring the worried words of Dr Wilcox as I go. I also ignore his receptionist as I hurry past her desk, not stopping to answer her queries about future appointments or the need to sign some paperwork.

Bursting through the front door, it feels good to be back in the fresh air, and I breathe in lungfuls of the stuff as I continue on down the street towards where I parked my car. As I go, I wonder which estimate on how long I have left will be right. Six months or twelve? But by the time I reach my car, I realise that it doesn't really matter. Either way, this time next year, I won't be alive. I won't be able to walk down this street or any other one. I won't be able to drive this car or sit in a passenger seat while somebody else drives for me. And I won't be able to talk to anybody, or smile, or kiss them, or do anything that human beings like to do to express their feelings.

I'll be in the ground. Just bones and dust.

Just another statistic.

I hope Dr Wilcox is wrong about my prognosis, but he is right about one thing. I should call somebody. This is way too much for me to deal with on my own.

Getting behind the wheel and closing the door, I decide to take out my phone and do just that, dialling the number of the person who deserves to hear this first.

As it rings, I wonder if they will pick up. But to my surprise, they do.

'Hi Claire,' I say. 'Is this a good time?'

'Erm…'

The confused hesitation from the other end of the line is nothing less than I expected, so I press on.

'It's just that you were kind enough to give me some news when you told me about what you had been doing with my husband, so I thought I'd return the favour. Here's my news. I'm dying. I've got less than a year. How does that make you feel?'

'Are you serious?'

'Deadly.'

'Oh my gosh, Alison. That's awful. I'm so sorry.'

I pretend like her words mean something to me even though they don't before saying what I really called her to say.

'I just thought you should know. I hope you feel guilty about what you have done to me, and if you didn't, then maybe you will now.'

'Is that why you called me? To make me feel bad?'

'No. I called you to let you know that I'm going to be gone soon, so Graham is going to be available again. I'm not sure if you still want him, but if you do, then you don't have to worry about me anymore.'

There's silence from the other end of the line, and I expect it's because Claire is trying to figure out why I am offering her my husband.

'Are you still there?' I ask, filling the quiet void.

'Yeah. I just don't know what to say. I thought you hated me.'

'Of course I hate you. You're a backstabbing bitch. But I'm dying, so I don't have time for petty emotions like that anymore. I also don't have time for my husband either. But the thing is, he won't leave me alone because he thinks there is a chance he can get back with me. Maybe he really loves me or maybe it's because he thinks he'll have no one if he doesn't have me. But if you were to let him know that you were still around, perhaps he would stop pestering me and leave me to die in peace.'

'You want me to start seeing your husband again?'

'I don't think it would do any harm at this point if you wanted to, yes.'

'But he chose you. That's why I did what I did. I was angry at him.'

'I get that but what's done is done. We can't change the past, but we can change our future. So how about it?'

'I don't know. This is weird.'

'It is, isn't it? So that's why I'm going to go. You won't be hearing from me again. But think about what I said. If you still have feelings for my husband, then you are free to do something about it. I don't care anymore. I have bigger things to worry about.'

With that, I hang up the phone and toss it onto the seat beside me before starting the engine and setting off in the direction of home. I turn on the radio as I go and purposefully go in search of a happy song to cheer myself up. All I want to do is cry and feel sorry for myself, but I know that won't help me accomplish any of the things that I need to do before my time on this earth is over.

I need to stay active, happy and focused.

Cancer might be the thing that the world believes is going to kill me.

But I could always make it look like something else instead.

16

GRAHAM

I still haven't given up on my marriage. Even now as I pack away my sleeping bag and hide away under my desk after the conclusion of my third night in a row of sleeping in my office at work. Yes, it's been three weeks since my wife found out about my affair, and she still hasn't let me know if she is willing to give me another chance, but I'm holding out hope. Maybe I'm deluded, and it could certainly look that way as I get changed out of my scruffy t-shirt and shorts and put my suit and tie on, now forced into dressing at work instead of at home in a bedroom like normal people do.

The hotel started getting a little too expensive after so long there, as well as a little too familiar. You know you've been staying there too long when the cleaners start asking you about your day, and the barmen already have your favourite drink ready before you've even sat down. After checking myself out, I tried again with Alison to see if there was any chance that she would allow me back home, telling her that I was willing to sleep in the spare bedroom or even on the couch, as long as it meant that I got to be nearer to her so we could talk. But she said no, so here I am, slumming it in the office and praying that none of my colleagues find out what I'm doing in case I get a warning from HR or just several sympathetic looks in the staffroom.

Fastening up the buttons on my crumpled white shirt, I check my reflection by using the selfie mode on my phone's camera and realise that I look even worse than I feel. My hair is sticking up all over the place, and I could do with a shave. A quick sniff under my armpit also lets me know that I could do with a shower.

This is stupid. I can't go on living like this. I know that I did wrong and accept that I should be punished for that, but there's a difference between feeling like I've lost something and having to live like a tramp. The time has come for me to force Alison into a decision, even if it turns out to be one that I don't agree with. If she is not going to take me back, I need to stop wasting my time and get myself set up somewhere proper. I'm done with hotels, and even though it's only been a few nights, I'm definitely done with sleeping at work.

Turning off the camera on my phone so I no longer have to look at my dishevelled appearance, I find Alison's number and give her a call. It's half past seven, so I expect her to be awake because she's always been a morning person, although I'm not sure what state she will be in on this particular day. She might be getting ready for work, or she might be recuperating at home, depending on how her treatment is going. That's the thing. I have absolutely no idea because she won't tell me what the current situation is regarding her illness. I have asked her in several text messages over these last few weeks for an update, but all she told me was that surgery went well, and she is discussing treatment options with her doctor now. But that's very vague.

Is she having chemo or not?

Is she out of the woods, or is this still a life-threatening battle that she faces?

Basically, I want to know if she is going to live or if there is still a chance she might die.

As her husband, I have a right to know that, even if I did stray and break her heart. That's why I am now going to keep calling and calling until she answers me and gives me a proper update on her health. Hopefully, she will give me an update on us then too.

My first attempt at speaking to her goes to voicemail, but I try again and again until Alison finally picks up at the fourth time of trying.

'What?' she asks me, her voice sounding weary and distant.

I'm not sure if that is because it's early in the morning or because she is struggling with the after-effects of whatever treatment she is being given.

'Hi. Thanks for picking up. I'm just calling because I'm worried about you, and I want to know what is happening.'

'I'm fine.'

She doesn't sound fine.

'Are you having chemo?' I ask, cutting straight to the chase.

'No, I'm not,' she replies, which sounds very promising even though the lack of energy in her voice is still troubling me.

'That's great!' I say. 'So you're going to be okay?'

'Why do you care?'

'Of course I care. You're my wife, and I'm worried about you.'

I expect to get more of a chance to remind her how much she means to me, but she changes the subject quickly.

'Where are you?'

I consider telling a lie and pretending that I'm still at the hotel, but I decide against it, mainly because it's lying that got me into this mess. Only the truth has a chance of getting me out of it.

'I'm at the office.'

'That's an early start.'

'I slept here last night.'

'Oh.'

Alison is obviously shocked at my admission, and I wonder if she is feeling sorry enough for me now to invite me back home, so I press on just to increase my chances.

‘Yeah. I’ve been sleeping here for the last few nights. The hotel is too expensive, and I got sick of hearing all the people in the rooms next to me jumping up and down on the beds or whatever it was that they were doing.’

I’m hoping a little humour about the couples I have overheard having sex recently is going to go some way to warming up the frosty atmosphere between us, but I hear no sign of laughter from the other end of the line.

‘Okay, well, if there’s nothing else, then I better get to work.’

‘You’re going into work?’

‘Yes, it is Wednesday.’

‘I know, but I just thought you might be resting.’

‘You thought I might be resting, so you decided to call me at half seven in the morning?’

‘You know what I mean. I knew you’d be up. You always were a morning person.’

‘And you always were a good husband. Right up until the time you suddenly stopped.’

Ouch. I’m not sure what the best thing to say to that is, so I say nothing at all.

‘I’m going to hang up now.’

'Alison, wait,' I beg, and my tone must be desperate enough to stop her from pressing the 'End Call' button on her mobile.

'What?'

'I can't do this anymore. I'm sorry, and I have been a bad husband, but I deserve to know where I stand. Are you going to give me another chance? I need to know because I can't go on sleeping in my office.'

'Oh, I'm sorry. I didn't realise you were waiting for an update from me,' Alison says, but I already know this isn't going to end well because she has that lilt to her voice that she always used to get when she was annoyed with me. 'How terrible of me to keep you waiting. I'm such a bad wife. You deserve so much better.'

Now she is obviously being sarcastic, which is only making me feel worse.

'Let me spell it out for you, so you are no longer in any doubt,' Alison says, and I brace myself for what is inevitably about to come next. 'We are finished. F-I-N-I-S-H-E-D. That means you are not going to be moving back into this house, nor are you and I ever going to share the same bed again. How's that for an update? Are you clear enough now?'

My fingers grip my mobile tightly as I do my best not to overreact and say something I might regret. Not only do I not want to make this conversation or my situation any worse, but I also don't want to give her the satisfaction of hearing me get angry.

If she really means what she has just said, then I guess that's it. We are over, and nothing I can say is going to change her mind now.

'Fine,' I reply through gritted teeth. 'At least I know where I stand. I guess I'll contact our lawyer and start the divorce process then.'

I wonder if that word might spark something in my wife and get her to reconsider, but it doesn't. She remains true to what she just told me.

'You do that,' she tells me. 'But don't expect him to take your side. Cheating spouses never do well in divorce settlements, and this time will be no different. I'm going to take you to the cleaners, and by the time I'm done with you, you're going to be glad you've got your office floor to sleep on because you sure as hell aren't going to be able to afford anywhere else.'

17

ALISON

It felt good to let off some steam at my husband and put him firmly in his place. He can have no doubt about where he stands now. We are finished, and he is going to have to face up to that fact. But if he thinks that my little outburst over the phone was brutal and cruel, then he better prepare himself for what is to come next because I haven't even got started on him yet.

If he thinks this is hell, wait until he sees where I am going to take him.

But there was an important omission from my conversation with Graham. I have not yet told him about my terminal diagnosis, and while I expect him to find out about it very soon, it's better if he doesn't hear it from me. That way it will be even more shocking when he does.

Even with the weight of the world on my shoulders, I still manage to give a wry smile when I think about Graham and the emotional rollercoaster that I am preparing to take him on. I also like the fact that he has been forced to sleep in his office. That was very amusing to me and is the least he deserves. He can't expect to climb back into our marital bed when he spent so long climbing into somebody else's.

I could stand there for longer and think about my husband shuffling in a sleeping bag under his desk, but I don't have time because I see the man walking down the street whom I have been waiting for. He is wearing a sharp suit, and I catch a glimpse of an expensive watch on his wrist, which reinforces how well he must be doing these days. Then again, I already knew that because I'd done a little digging online before today. I know that this man is now Head of Corporate Strategy at an investment company with offices all over the world, and while I have no idea what that kind of job entails, I'm guessing it pays very well. That could be why he has a big grin on his face as he makes his way towards his expensive car, or maybe it's because he is setting up another hot date with one of his many women as he texts on his phone.

Either way, I'm about to give him something else to smile about.

Leaving my hiding place on the street corner, I walk out across the pavement and into full view of the man coming towards me, and I've timed it well enough so that I am able to catch him before he climbs behind the wheel of his vehicle.

'Andy? I thought it was you!'

I might be overdoing it a little on the shock levels, but I'm not an actress needing to convince a panel of Oscar judges. I just need to make this man think that my bumping into him has been a coincidence. And I must do a good enough job of it because he looks just as surprised as I am pretending to be.

'Alison! Wow, I didn't realise it was you.'

I know that isn't a lie because if he had seen me coming, then he almost certainly would have ducked out of view. That's because I can't imagine there are too many men who would want to bump into their ex-wife's best friend.

Andy is Claire's ex-husband, the one whom she would regularly fantasise about killing during our coffee catch-ups. Now they are divorced, and from what I've heard, Andy has fully embraced his newfound single life, making even more of a mockery of the fact that he once stood in front of a large congregation and repeated vows that made it seem like he was a one-woman man for the rest of his life.

He definitely looks nervous now as he stands here in front of me, and he is probably wondering if he is going to get a load of abuse from me in defence of Claire, even though it has been a long time since they separated. After all, he still thinks I'm her best friend, so he will know I will always take her side. But he is wrong about that now.

'Good to see you again. How are you? You look like you're doing well!' I say, making a big show of eyeing him up and down before letting my eyes settle on his car parked beside us.

'Err, yeah. Things are okay,' he says, clearly confused. 'How are you?'

'Well, let's just say that a lot has happened to me recently, and not all of it has been good, but I'm still plodding on.'

'Oh, okay. Great.'

It's endearing how nervous he is, and I can see him glancing behind me as if he is worried that his ex-wife is somewhere in the vicinity too.

'Don't worry, Claire's not with me,' I say, putting him at ease, and he laughs, albeit very awkwardly.

'How is she?'

'I don't care,' I reply, making Andy even more confused.

'You don't?'

'Nope. We're not friends anymore. Not since she had an affair with Graham, anyway.'

'She did what?'

Andy's eyes are wide with shock, and I wonder if that's what I looked like when Claire dropped the news on me on my doorstep a few weeks ago. Probably.

'Her and Graham had a fling. It might still be going on now, I'm not sure. But I kicked him out obviously, and I haven't seen her either.'

'I'm really sorry to hear that,' Andy offers, and I thank him, even if it is a little strange to hear an adulterer offer sympathy for someone else's adultery.

'That's not all,' I say, preparing to hit him with the double-whammy of shocking news. 'I've also got cancer, and it's terminal. I'm going to be dead in a year.'

Andy looks like he could fall over as he processes what I am telling him before he reaches out a hand and rests it on my arm to provide support to me.

'Oh Alison, I'm so sorry. That's awful.'

'Yeah, it is,' I say before shrugging so that I don't bring the vibe between us down too much. 'But I guess one good thing about it is that it has brought everything into sharper focus, do you know what I mean?'

Andy nods even though he probably has no idea what I mean.

'Like my husband's affair with Claire. I would have probably spent the last few weeks crying into my pillow and feeling sorry for myself, but it's forcing me to get out and get on with things while I still can.'

Andy nods again.

'It's also made me want to do everything I've thought about doing,' I say, looking Andy right in the eye. 'Like you, I suppose.'

'P-p-pardon?' Andy stutters, presumably wondering if he just heard me right.

'I've always thought about what it would be like to be with you,' I tell him, smiling suggestively. 'Obviously, I never would have acted on it when I was with Graham or when you were with Claire, but as neither of those people are in our lives anymore, I have been thinking about it more and more.'

Andy looks like he has no idea what to say to that, so I do the talking for him.

'Basically, I'm dying, and I want to have as much fun as I can before I go. So how about it? Me and you? Let's have some fun.'

Andy looks puzzled and glances behind me again as if he is expecting this to be all some kind of practical joke. But I keep the smile on my face to let him know that I am serious.

'I don't know what to say.'

'Say yes, and let's go back to your place.'

Andy realises then that I am deadly serious, so he wastes no time in making his decision based on that.

'Err, okay. Get in.'

He rushes around to the driver side door of his vehicle, almost as if he doesn't want to risk me changing my mind, but I'm not about to do that.

Instead, I simply slide into the passenger seat beside him and give him another smile as he starts the engine and sets off in the direction of his home in anticipation of a spontaneous afternoon with his ex-wife's ex-best friend.

I bet he never thought he would find himself in this situation.

He isn't the only one.

18

GRAHAM

After what Alison said to me over the phone this morning, I guess I should call my lawyer. But I have found myself dialling somebody else's number instead.

I'm calling Claire.

As I wait for her to pick up, I'm not entirely sure what I hope to get out of this upcoming conversation. But the fact that I have decided to call her after learning that my marriage is definitely over should tell me that my intentions aren't exactly honourable. I can try and pretend to myself that I am just contacting her to see how she is doing, which would be a perfectly legitimate thing to do considering how close we once were. But really, I suspect I am doing it because I want to see if there is any chance that we can rekindle what we had together, so I don't end up losing both my wife and my lover and making this whole sorry affair a total disaster on my part.

While I was prepared to fight for Alison and try and save my marriage, I am not prepared for starting again at my age without anybody. After my affair was unearthed, I chose Alison. But if I can't be with her, then I guess I choose Claire.

The only problem is, I'm not sure if she is going to be receptive to that now that she knows she is second best.

'What do you want?'

Claire's greeting over the phone is as warm and welcoming as one might expect to get when they have been treated terribly, and it's the least that I deserve.

'Claire. Hi. I'm just calling to say sorry and make sure you are okay.'

'Save your breath,' she snaps back, and I'm worried she is going to hang up right there, but she allows me the chance to speak again.

'I'm also calling to say that I've made a mistake.'

'What do you mean?'

'I should never have said that I would choose Alison over you. That was stupid of me. Of course I choose you. You're the one I really want to be with. That's obvious. Why else would I have behaved the way I did if I was happy with her?'

There is silence down the line, and I can only hope it is a good sign that means Claire is taking on board what I am saying to her.

'I've been an idiot,' I go on. 'I know that now. But I hope it isn't too late for us. I think we can still be together. Don't you?'

I've taken my shot, and now all I can do is wait to see what the outcome will be. Will Claire tell me to get lost like my wife did? Or will she give me the chance that I need to get my life back on some kind of track and keep me from sleeping on this damn office floor for the foreseeable future?

But when her reaction comes, it's not at all what I am expecting.

'You're despicable,' she says to me, the venom in her voice startling me and being far worse than anything I might have expected to hear from her after my pitch to save our relationship.

'Excuse me?'

'You heard me. You're despicable. Disgusting. I don't even know what I ever saw in you.'

Then the line goes dead, abruptly ending the call before I have a chance to find out what has got Claire so riled.

I stare at my phone in disbelief. I knew it wasn't going to be easy to get Claire back on side after I ditched her for Alison, but I did not expect that reaction. That wasn't just anger or frustration. That was sheer hatred, or worse, disgust, just like she said.

But why? She can't hate me that much, surely?

I need more answers, so I try calling her back again, but she doesn't pick up, and I'm still left in the dark. Worse, I'm still left facing the possibility of being on my own, without either my wife or my lover.

I have made a right mess of this and only have myself to blame, but I don't have much time to feel sorry for myself because the door to my office swings open and one of my colleagues walks in.

'Graham! How are you doing on that analytics report for McKenzie?'

This is Kevin, my boss and a man I do not want to disappoint, which is a problem because I'm going to have to. That's because I haven't finished the report yet due to the fact that I have been far too preoccupied with trying to salvage something with either of the two women in my life. But that's not going to be much of an excuse to give to Kevin, so I better think of something else fast before I lose this job and with that, my best chance of a bed for the night.

'It's almost done. I could just use one more day to play around with the numbers a little bit,' I try, hoping that will be good enough. But it's not.

'You've got an hour,' Kevin snaps back. 'That report was due yesterday.'

With that, he turns and walks out of the office, no doubt on his way to see somebody else about something they haven't delivered to him in time. But at least he has given me a chance, and while an hour isn't enough, it's better than nothing.

I can work with that, and it should mean I won't be getting fired today, which is one less problem to have to think about.

As I put my phone down and get to work on my computer, I do my best to forget all about my hectic personal life and instead focus on my professional one. If I can't get things right with women, at least I can do my best to get things right here with several men, all of whom will be waiting for this report so they can sit in an extremely stuffy boardroom and pore over it while making all sorts of projections and conclusions.

But I'm barely ten minutes into my work when my phone rings again, and even though I know I should just leave it because I really need to get this report finished, I can't help but pick up when I see the caller I.D.

It's Claire.

Maybe she has calmed down and is calling back to apologise to me. I guess she has realised that she might have overreacted, and maybe she has even had time to reconsider the fact that she doesn't have to be alone either. She can take me back, and all of this nonsense can be over.

With that optimistic thought in mind, I answer the phone quickly.

'Hi.'

'I just wanted to say that you really are the lowest of the low.'

'What?'

'It's funny. I used to feel sorry for you and hate your wife for making you unhappy, but now it's her who I feel bad for. And myself. Both of us did not deserve to be with a man as selfish as you.'

'Calm down.'

'No, I will not calm down! I'm fuming! And I bet Alison is too. You've lied to both of us, and now you are jumping from one ship to another simply because it's what's best for you, without giving a damn about either of our feelings.'

'Did you just call me back to have another go at me? Because if so, then I don't want to hear it. I just thought I'd let you know that I was missing you, but if you're going to be like this, then I wish I hadn't bothered.'

'Oh, I bet you wish you hadn't bothered now you know that I know about Alison's diagnosis too.'

'This has nothing to do with her cancer.'

'Stop lying! It's why you're calling me, isn't it? You chose a sick person, and now you regret it, so you're going with me simply because I'm the healthy one. That's disgraceful.'

All this time, I thought Claire was mad at me simply because I chose Alison first. But now it seems like she has this belief that I'm changing my mind and choosing my mistress because she is cancer-free.

'That's not why I've changed my mind,' I say, doing my best to be persuasive. 'It's because I really want to be with you.'

'Don't make me laugh. You just don't want to be by yourself. Now your wife is dying, you suddenly want me. What a shock! I hate you!'

'Alison isn't dying,' I say. 'She is having treatment, but she is going to be okay.'

There's a pause down the line, and I'm not sure why but I wonder if I have managed to say something that might help me. But then Claire speaks again.

'Now you're not just being selfish. You're being delusional.'

'What?'

'Alison is dying. She told me so.'

'Why would she do that?'

'I don't know but she did!'

I think about it for a moment, but it doesn't make any sense. Yes, my wife has cancer but it's way too early to tell how bad it is. Or is it? She hasn't told me about it recently and maybe this is why.

'What did Alison say exactly?' I ask.

'Don't play dumb with me,' Claire hisses back.

'I'm not!'

'She told me she has less than a year to live. She obviously wanted to make me feel even more guilty about things. But that's why you called me today, isn't it? You found out there is no chance Alison survives this, so you have backtracked on your decision and want me instead.'

That's not at all what has happened here, but I'm not bothered about defending myself. I'm more concerned about the fact that Alison has told Claire that she only has a year to live.

Is that true?

Is my wife really dying?

If so, why the hell hasn't she told me?

19

ALISON

I had thought it would be awkward to kiss a man who wasn't my husband after so many years of faithful wedlock on my part. Maybe it would have been if things had been normal, and I'd have time for silly things like doubt, guilt and being self-conscious. But things are definitely not normal, and now I have a maximum of twelve months to live, I certainly don't have time for things like that. The only thing I do have time for these days is action. Firm, decisive action. And that's exactly what has just happened.

Andy and I took action.

Plenty of it.

I'm still lying in his bed beside him as we recover from all that action, breathless and beaming as if we know we have just done something we shouldn't have, but boy did it feel good. I imagine Andy is feeling rather happy with himself, getting to add another notch to his busy bedpost and his ex-wife's best friend no less, while I suspect he thinks I am just as happy having now got revenge on both Graham and Claire, mentally at least. But he would be wrong. I haven't got my revenge yet. The sex was merely a precursor for what is to really come.

I look towards the curtains that Andy pulled closed just seconds before we fell into bed together, and I see no evidence of sunlight seeping through them anymore. It's dark out there now, which is good. But I can't lie here all night. The clock is ticking down on my life, and I feel like I can almost hear the second hands going by in my head with every precious little moment that I waste doing nothing.

'Can I use your shower?' I ask the naked Andy as he continues to lie on his back beside me.

'Sure. You want company in there?'

I smile because I was wondering if he would make that suggestion.

'Give me five minutes, then come and join me,' I tell him, and the wide grin on his face lets me know what he thinks about that idea.

Pulling back the duvet, I feel the heat quickly escape my body, and I waste little time hopping out of the bed and scooping up a few of my things, including my handbag, before I go into the bathroom and close the door.

Making sure to leave it unlocked, I put my handbag on the marble sink and take a look at my reflection in the mirror. I'm hardly looking my best right now after rolling around in a bed for the last hour, but I don't look bad either. I certainly don't look like I'm dying, which is both a good thing and a bad thing. It's good because hopefully, it will be a while before I start to lose a lot of weight and gradually look more drawn and haggard as my body fights a losing battle. But it's also slightly annoying because it seems so ridiculous that I have been told I only have a year to live when on the surface, it appears like I am in full health. But there's no time for feeling sorry for myself. There will come a day when I get to contemplate all of this and possibly lament how unfair everything has been. But not today.

Today, I have to keep a brave face on.

With that in mind, I refocus and turn around to the shower, noting how large and most likely expensive it is. It's not just Andy's suit, watch and car that proves he is doing well since Claire threw him out after he cheated. His new home proves it too.

Andy now lives in a large detached house in an affluent suburb of this town, and the interior is very stylishly decorated, although I expect he just paid somebody to do it all for him rather than spending time fussing over fabrics and countertops himself. It does seem rather a waste for him to have this whole place to himself without a wife to share it with, but then I know he has never been short of female company, so I'm sure he manages just fine. And to think that Graham and I used to go on double dates with him and Claire, sitting together in restaurants and talking about things that couples do. We've all come a long way since then.

Technically, every single one of us has cheated on the others. Andy cheated on Claire. Her and Graham cheated on me. And now I have cheated on Graham because I'm still legally married to him even if we are now estranged.

What a wild bunch we are. The famous four.

But we'll be the infamous four by the time I'm finished.

Reaching out for the handle that I assume controls the shower, I turn it on and a strong jet of water bursts out from the head, hitting the tray and running away quickly down the plughole. I make sure to make a loud point of sliding the shower door open and closed before stepping back and watching the glass door steam up as the hot water continues to pour.

Then I return to my handbag and quickly locate the item I placed in there before I met Andy this afternoon. Taking it out, I crawl underneath the marble countertop that holds the sink, making sure that I will be out of the view of the homeowner when he comes in here in a moment's time.

As I crouch in position, my breathing steady and the temperature in here rising, I think about how none of this would be happening if Dr Wilcox had given me better news the other day. If I wasn't dying, then I wouldn't be in this house now, lurking with intent, preparing to do something that wouldn't look out of place in a television show about dangerous people. I'd probably just be like so many other broken-hearted women in the world. Sad, lonely and filling my time with bad chick-flicks, wine and a promise that I will never be walked over by a man again. But thanks to that bad news, I'm here, naked, satisfied and focused.

It's funny how life is.

The sound of the door handle turning causes me to remain still as I prepare for Andy to enter the steamy bathroom.

'Wow, it's hot in here,' he says as he walks in and closes the door behind him. I can only see his bare feet and ankles from my hiding place, but I assume that the rest of him is just as exposed right now. 'I have a feeling it's going to get even hotter.'

I cringe at his lame joke as I watch his feet walk over to the shower door, and now it's almost time.

'Ready or not, here I come,' he calls before opening the door and stepping inside the spacious and steamy shower. But before he has a chance to realise that I'm not in there waiting for him, I leave my hiding place and rush forward, the knife in my hand raised above my head.

Andy must have either seen that the shower was empty or sensed me approaching from behind because he turns around and looks right at me. But it's too late for him to stop what I am about to do.

I plunge the knife into the side of his neck, seeing the wide whites of his eyes as the deadly weapon punctures his skin and draws an ungodly amount of blood.

Figuring that one blow might not be enough, I stab the knife into his naked body another four times before he eventually slips and falls to the shower floor, the clean water mixing in with the dirty blood as it all washes away quickly down the plughole.

He reaches out for the slippery wall beside him to presumably try and get back to his feet before I can rain any more blows down upon him, but he finds no purchase there and slips further under the jet of hot water.

I consider stabbing him again just to make sure, but then I notice that his eyes are closed, and his body is motionless. Watching him for a few moments, I see no further signs of life. The water still runs over him, and his blood still runs away, but he is no longer moving.

I've done it.

I've killed Andy.

Now I just need to get away with it.

Step one of that plan involves me getting clean, so I close the shower door behind me and make sure to wash myself, scrubbing and rinsing until I am as clean as can be. Then I remove the showerhead from its holder and run it all over Andy's lifeless body, washing away any of my hairs that may have fallen on to it during our time together.

When I am convinced that he is clean enough, barring the bloody stab wounds that are still leaking, of course, I turn the shower off and step out, reaching for a towel on the heated rack and drying off quickly. Then I re-enter the bedroom and get dressed before returning to the bathroom to pick up my handbag, take the towel and make sure I have left nothing behind in this steamy room of death.

My last job before I leave is to take the bedsheets and pillowcases off and put them in Andy's washing machine, along with a few items of clothing that I find in his wardrobe. I don't want the police to know that he had another woman in his bed this evening, and the heated spin cycle now cleansing the bed linen should take care of that. The presence of the clothes alongside them should mean it just looks like the man put on a wash load, instead of what it really is, which is a killer cleaning any evidence of her presence here.

As I leave the washing machine to work its magic, I head for the door, happy now that this place looks exactly how I want it to when the police eventually come in here.

A tidy house, as it should be.

Clean items in the washing machine as if it was just a normal night of chores.

And the dead body in the shower, looking like an intruder came in and caught the homeowner when he least expected it before stabbing him to death.

The police will conclude that he never stood a chance, and they would be right.

But he's not the only one who didn't have a chance.

The person I am going to frame for his murder doesn't have one either.

20

GRAHAM

I know I shouldn't have snuck into the house without Alison being here, but technically, this is still my home, and I am paying half the mortgage, so I have a right to use my key and walk inside. Of course, it would have been easier if Alison had just answered the door when I knocked on it upon my arrival ten minutes ago, but she isn't home, so I had no choice but to come inside. I need to speak to her, and I am not leaving here until I do.

But where is she?

It's gone eight, and there is no sign of her. I doubt she has been going into work considering the bad news she has just got, and even if she has, she would never normally stay there this late. I wonder if she is at the hospital, having some treatment or just another meeting with her doctor. That will be my next place to check, but I'd rather I didn't have to go hunting for her all over town. I'd rather she was here so we could have this conversation in the privacy of our own home.

I try her mobile again, but it's still turned off, so I sit down on the sofa and turn the TV on.

For a second, it almost feels as if everything is normal, and I am just a husband sitting at home relaxing while waiting for his wife to join him. If only. Instead, I feel like an intruder because I know Alison wants me out and would go mad if she found me here. But I'm determined to talk to her and find out if what Claire said to me earlier is true.

I need to know if my wife is dying, and I need to hear it from her.

Flicking through several channels, all of which remind me of how bad TV has gotten these days, I eventually get restless and turn it off again before getting up and going into the kitchen. I'm starving, but somehow, I think cooking a meal might be pushing my luck too far, considering I shouldn't be here. I don't think Alison would be impressed to come home and find her cheating husband standing in front of a boiling pot of pasta with an apron on and a spatula in hand. But while cooking might be off-limits, I'm sure a beer isn't out of the question. I just hope Alison hasn't thrown them all out since I have been gone.

Rummaging around in the fridge, I get lucky and find a cold bottle at the back, hidden amongst all the salad and vegetables that my wife loved to eat, although her healthy diet now seems a little pointless if the news of her terrible diagnosis is true.

Popping the cap on the bottle, I lean back against the kitchen counter and take a long sip of beer. I feel my eyes watering as I do, but it's not because of the cold liquid slipping down my throat. It's the thought that my poor wife might not have long to live, and soon, this house will be empty of her presence forever, regardless of what happens to our marriage.

Leaving the kitchen, I wander around fairly aimlessly through all the different rooms of the house, thinking back over the memories that this property holds for us ever since we moved into it just after our wedding day. The living room where we spent many a happy night curled up in each other's arms, watching a movie or two with a bottle of wine and the remnants of a takeaway on the table in front of us. The spare bedroom, which I sometimes used as a study, but she also used as a dressing room to store all her makeup and excess shoes. And the dining room, where we hosted several dinners with friends, including Claire and Andy, once a happy couple just like us but now separated, much like Alison and I are fated to be.

As I move through each room, the beer giving me refreshment as I go, I almost can't believe how stupid I was for putting everything at risk for a fling. Not only that, but I even thought that leaving Alison for Claire was the best thing for me. But now, as I walk around my home, I know how wrong I was. This is the best place for me, and Alison always was the best woman for me. What a fool I have been and what a waste of a perfectly good home to grow old in. I wonder who will live here after us, moving in and putting their own stamp on the property. They might redecorate the kitchen. They may even knock down that wall and make a bigger dining room like I had considered doing. And they will probably get better use out of that spare bedroom than we did, giving it a sole purpose rather than the dual one which we used it for that never really maximised its true potential. The new homeowners might even speculate about why we are selling it, probably figuring that we're separating and feeling sorry for us whilst believing that their relationship will never get to that unretrievable point. But they can't know that for sure. I certainly didn't. I moved in here thinking this was where I would live forever, growing old with Alison by my side, yet only a few years later, that is not the case.

I won't grow old here.

And sadly, it sounds like my wife won't either.

I hear the sound of a car engine outside and rush to the bedroom window, looking out and seeing Alison parking on the driveway. She's back from wherever she has been, and I'm glad because it means I won't have to go out looking for her. Instead, I can just go downstairs and get some answers right now.

I'm standing in the hallway when she comes through the front door, but I make sure to call out and let her know that I am here in case she gets startled. But she doesn't seem surprised. She tells me she noticed my car out front and presumed I was inside. I apologise for coming in while she was out but tell her that I needed to talk to her desperately. She asks me why, although I wonder if she already knows.

I tell her it's because I heard the cancer was worse than I thought, and then I ask her if it is true. Is she really dying?

Her answer is a solemn one.

Yes, it's true. She's dying.

That's when I start to cry. I can't help it.

She starts to cry too.

Then we hug. My intentions are pure, and I just want to comfort her, but after a few moments, I feel the atmosphere between us change, and I wonder if there is a chance of something more.

There is only one way to find out, but I don't want to ruin things, so I allow her to make the first move. Her lips meet mine, and now we are kissing. It feels awkward for a moment, mainly because it's been a while since we did this, but we soon get back into our old groove. But something is different. I can sense an energy in my wife that I have never felt before. She seems more urgent. More eager.

More alive.

I get confirmation of that when she declines my suggestion of going upstairs and instead leads me into the kitchen, where she proceeds to clear the table and let me know that this is where we are to do our making up tonight.

I wonder if I am taking advantage of her emotional state and hesitate for a moment, but then she pulls me towards her, and we are kissing again. Seconds later and I am on top of her on the table.

I wonder if it will hold us both.

It does.

I guess our marriage might not be over after all.

21

ALISON

Believe it or not, I wasn't planning on being intimate with my husband on the kitchen table as soon as I came home from killing Andy. I was rather expecting to have the house to myself considering that Graham should not have been here. But there he was, asking me about my diagnosis, having obviously heard about it from Claire. I had wanted to know if the pair of them were still in contact with each other, which is why I told her about my terminal diagnosis and not him. The fact that he knew gave me my answer about the two of them still talking.

Maybe it was all the adrenaline of what I had just done with Andy, or perhaps it was the emotion of hearing the man I once loved asking me if I was dying, but we ended up hugging, then kissing, then ultimately having sex.

Now the intimacy has come to an end, at least physically, and we are both sitting on the kitchen floor, half-naked and out of breath, looking at each other and wondering what the hell just happened.

'Wow,' Graham says after allowing a few more moments for us both to get our heart rate back down.

'Indeed,' I reply because that's all I can offer at this stage.

Then we both burst out laughing, the awkward atmosphere cut instantly and putting us more at ease.

'So, where do we stand?' Graham asks when we finally stop laughing.

That's a good question and one I would like to have more time to think about, but as Dr Wilcox so brutally informed me, time is not on my side. With that in mind, I try to make the best out of this situation. What happened with Andy was part of my plan but what just happened on this kitchen table was not. But that's okay. I can improvise and adapt as well as anybody.

'I'm not sure,' I say. 'My head's all over the place.'

'I understand. But I wish you'd told me about your diagnosis sooner.'

'It's been difficult.'

'Why did you tell Claire and not me?'

'I guess I wanted her to feel guilty about what she did to me.'

'And you didn't want me to feel guilty?'

'I already knew you did.'

‘You still should have told me. I’m still your husband, despite what has happened.’

‘You’re right. I’m sorry.’

‘You’re not the one who has anything to apologise for.’

That is true as far as Graham is concerned, but I guess Andy might say otherwise if he was still alive now.

I decide to get up off the kitchen floor, mainly because it’s a ridiculous place to sit and hold a conversation, before telling Graham that he should go. But he’s not happy about that.

‘Come on, Alison,’ he says as we both start putting the rest of our clothes back on. ‘Let’s sort this out. I want to be here to help you, but I can’t be if you’re not letting me stay in the house.’

‘I don’t need your help,’ I reply defiantly, and I mean it, even if I’m not sure exactly what is coming for me further down the road when my health deteriorates.

‘I just want to be here to give you support. You shouldn’t be going through this alone.’

‘I wouldn’t be if you hadn’t started an affair with my best friend.’

‘What I did was wrong. I know that,’ Graham admits. ‘And I deserved to be punished. But I also deserve a second chance, don’t I? Or does one mistake cancel out years of marriage?’

Calling an affair “one mistake” is laughable, but I don’t say that because I can see that Graham is genuinely sorry for what he has done to me. But I also know he would say anything right now not to have to go back to sleeping on his office floor, so I need to be cautious.

‘Why do you want to be with me instead of her?’ I ask as I finish getting dressed and go over to the sink to pour myself a cup of water.

‘Because I love you,’ he tells me.

‘And you don’t love her?’

‘I thought I did. But I don’t. Not like I love you.’

‘So you’d really rather be with me?’

‘Yes.’

‘Even though I’m dying?’

‘Of course.’

I take a long sip of water as I watch Graham finish getting dressed, and I wonder how hard he tried to make a go of things with Claire before she knocked him back again and he realised that I was his best bet for companionship. Considering how well I know this man and what he is like, it’s embarrassing that I really never saw his affair coming.

I’m just glad I found out about it before I was gone. It would have been too late then to exact my revenge.

'What are you thinking?' Graham asks me as he comes closer and puts a hand on my arm.

I consider being honest and telling him that I am fantasising about how I am going to get my own back, but that wouldn't be prudent, so I just decide to take a leaf out of his book and lie instead.

'I'm thinking about all the things I wanted to do before I died,' I say, doing my best to bring a few tears to my eyes for dramatic effect. 'All those plans. Gone.'

'You still have time,' Graham says, looking almost as upset as I am pretending to be.

'Maybe.'

I wipe a tear from my eye before Graham pulls me in for a hug and comforts me, but all I can think about is getting on with the next part of my plan. It's funny, but maybe his affair with Claire has been the best thing that could have happened to me regarding my diagnosis. Without the motivation and drive it has given me to seek revenge, I dread to think how listless and depressing my existence would be now. As it is, I'm not thinking about the bleakness of death all day. Instead, I'm excited by the future, however short it may be, because I have much to accomplish and much satisfaction to gain from seeing Graham and Claire suffer.

'How about I move back in on a trial basis?' Graham suggests as he continues to hug me tightly.

'Spare bedroom, of course. And I'll leave you alone unless you want to talk to me.'

He's trying his luck, but fair play to him; you don't get anything if you don't ask.

I decide that as much as fun as it would be for me to make him sleep at his office for a few more nights yet, it won't make too much of a difference if I let him come home now. I've played with him enough already, even though I've barely gotten started. There's so much more to come, and now he is back under the same roof as me, I'm going to see his reaction to it all as it unfolds right in front of his eyes.

Just like Andy an hour ago in his shower, my poor husband isn't going to know what has hit him until it's too late.

22

GRAHAM

I've made plenty of mistakes, and I'm not the perfect man, but maybe this is where I get to make things right. Now I'm allowed back home again, I can be the one to care for Alison and guide her through her illness, giving her all the strength that she needs before she eventually loses her battle and slips away. Maybe that doesn't make up for breaking her heart, but I can't change the past. All I can do now is focus on the future, which is why I will go and see what I can do to help in a moment just as soon as I have finished unpacking my things into the spare bedroom.

Yesterday was quite the rollercoaster, starting with me waking up in my office, then finding out about Alison's diagnosis from Claire, before it ended in Alison and I making love on the kitchen table, and her agreeing to let me come back home. That's quite a twenty-four hours to wrap my head around, but thankfully, today has been quieter, and apart from packing up my sleeping bag and bringing it back here, there have been no dramas to report.

It's a relief to be back home now and have a proper bed to sleep on, even if I will still be sleeping alone for the foreseeable future. Alison will be sleeping on the other side of this wall, so close yet so far, but that's okay because she still needs time, and I will give her as long as she wants. I know I'm fortunate to have this second chance. Most men who get caught cheating on their wives are turfed out from the family home, never to return again. But here I am, back in the building and hopefully working my way back into Alison's good books.

I'm just about to close the door of the wardrobe in which I have finished hanging a couple of my work shirts that I transferred back here from my office when I hear the notification on my mobile phone. The unique ringtone lets me know that it is a local police update, just another of the notifications that I signed up to receive a few years ago because it's the quickest way of knowing what is happening in the area. I signed up for them mainly to get any traffic updates, so I wouldn't get caught in any traffic jams on the way into work or on the way home, but they also send me updates about criminal investigations and any other items deemed newsworthy. I don't always bother to read them, but I could use a distraction today, so I walk over to my phone and pick it up before taking a seat on the bed and opening the app.

That's when I see a headline that I have never seen in this part of the world before.

LOCAL MAN FOUND MURDERED IN OWN HOME

I click the link to the main article, intrigued and shocked in equal measure. This is a small town, and while there are plenty of things wrong with it, one of them is not our serious crime rate. I don't ever recall somebody being murdered around here, which is why I'm interested in finding out exactly what has happened.

The first paragraph doesn't tell me much more than what the headline said, but then I see the name mentioned in the second paragraph, and that's when I'm glad that I took a seat before I started reading. If I hadn't, I'd have probably fallen over in shock because I know the victim this article is referring to.

It's Andy King.

Claire's ex-husband.

I quickly finish reading the article to learn more about what had happened to the poor man but other than mentioning that he was found at home after police were called when he failed to turn up for work, there is nothing to say the cause of death, although it is being treated as suspicious. Apparently, there are no suspects yet, but the scene is being combed for evidence, and the police hope to have more information soon. In the meantime, they are assuring the public that there is no wider risk to them, although that's not exactly comforting when somebody has been murdered, and they don't know who did it.

I can't believe that this has happened to somebody I used to know well. Andy and I sat across a table from each other several times besides our respective wives. Double dating, I believe they call it. While we weren't exactly the best of friends, we always got on well enough to prevent it from being awkward, and the fact that we both enjoyed a good glass or two of wine made things easier. Of course, it was Alison and Claire who were the reason we got together for meals and drinks, but I never used to mind catching up with Andy. He was a friendly guy, chatty and confident, if a little arrogant on occasion, although only after the second bottle of wine came out. But I haven't seen him for a long time, not since he cheated on Claire and they separated.

To say it was a shock at the time was an understatement. I had always considered them a stronger couple than Alison and I were, although admittedly, that was only an opinion formed during the couple of hours we got together once or twice a month. I guess things hadn't been so rosy behind closed doors, which is why Andy strayed, and I can understand that now in hindsight because I ended up doing the same thing as him in the end.

I doubt he ever found out that I had been intimate with his wife after they separated, and from what Claire had told me about him, Andy seemed to have moved on well enough in his life, thriving both at work and on the dating scene. But now he is dead. Murdered in his own home.

What the hell happened?

And I wonder if Claire knows about it yet?

I consider calling her and breaking the news, figuring that it might be easier for her to hear it from me rather than from someone else or the next time she decides to check the news websites online. I really hope she doesn't receive the same notifications as I do with the newsflashes because that would be a very shocking way for her to find out about her ex-husband's demise. But then I decide not to get in touch with her, one, because things are no longer good between the pair of us, and two, my wife is in the next room, and I don't want her to overhear me on the phone to my mistress just after she has let me back into the house.

Then I wonder if Alison has heard the news, so I decide to get up off the bed and go and speak to her.

Knocking on the closed bedroom door, I enter cautiously, unsure if my wife is sleeping or in any kind of pain from her recent treatment. But she is sitting up on the bed watching television, and right now, she almost looks as if everything is okay. But it's not, and what I am about to tell her is only going to make things worse.

'Have you heard the news?' I ask as I stand in the doorway, my mobile phone in my hand with the screen still showing the shocking article.

'What news?' Alison asks me, her eyes not moving from the television.

'Andy's dead. They think he was murdered.'

'What?'

Alison quickly turns the TV off and looks at me with a stunned expression that lets me know she needs to read this article quickly to avoid further confusion.

I rush over to the bed and hand the phone to her so she can see the news for herself, and she gasps as she reads the piece.

'Oh my god. This is awful.'

'I know. Who the hell would want to kill Andy?'

'I don't know.'

Alison scrolls through the article, but she isn't able to get any more answers than I was able to find when I read it a moment ago.

'Do you think the police will want to speak to us?' I ask my wife.

'Why would they want to do that?'

'Because we knew him. They might want help with establishing who might have done this.'

‘I don’t think we can be much help.’

‘Well, you never know.’

‘I know who might have had a reason to kill him.’

I pause because I’m surprised by Alison’s statement.

‘What do you mean by that?’ I ask her.

‘What do you think?’

I’m getting an idea of who she is referring to.

‘No way,’ I say. ‘She wouldn’t have done this.’

I shake my head again, refusing to even entertain the idea that Andy could have been killed by his ex-wife. The same woman I embarked on an affair with.

‘Claire didn’t do this. She isn’t a killer.’

Alison raises her eyebrows, and it almost looks like she is going to smile before she catches herself and speaks again.

‘You better hope that is the case,’ she says to me, turning the TV back on with the remote. ‘Otherwise, she might be coming for you next.’

23

ALISON

Andy's murder is all over the news, as it should be. It would be a shocking story anywhere, whether it occurred on the mean streets of New York or in the sleepy suburbs of some town that nobody has ever heard of. The newspapers, TV bulletins and radio broadcasts are full of mentions of the victim's name, as well as the fact that, as of yet, nobody has been charged with the heinous crime.

But I have a feeling that is about to change today.

Putting my nervous energy to good use, I left home armed with nothing but my handbag and the contents of my purse, determined to give myself a distraction from all the crazy goings on lately. Retail therapy is what's required, and that is exactly what I am giving myself now. It's no longer just my handbag slung over my arm. Now, there are four shopping bags alongside it, all accumulated from various stores in this sprawling shopping centre, and all filled with expensive clothes that looked great on me when I tried them on earlier. But I'm not done yet. I still want another dress, and I think I have found just the one.

Taking the slinky black number off the rack, I carry it towards the changing room, smiling at the pretty shop assistant as she gives me a number and shows me into one of the stalls where I will be afforded some privacy behind the blue curtain. Changing out of my rather dour outfit, I put on the more glamorous one, careful not to aggravate my wounds from my surgery a few weeks ago when my lump was originally removed. I'm still healing, although any recovery made will only be on a superficial level. Below the surface, things continue to get worse, and I will never be fully healed again. But that is why I am here now, buying clothes I can barely afford. Impending death has a funny way of making things like sensible spending seem totally pointless. Who cares what shopping bill I run up today? I'm not going to be around long enough to have to worry about it, that's for sure.

Smoothing down the dress on my hips, I examine my reflection in the mirror and feel pleased with my find. This is a stunning piece, no doubt about it, and it's certainly worthy of its hefty price tag. I expect most women who have frequented this shop recently have baulked when they saw the £1000 price tag attached to this dress, but I'm not most women.

I'm a woman whose days are numbered, which means I have nothing to lose, least of all money.

I wish I could just keep the dress on and walk out of here in it, but that's not how it works, so I make myself get changed again before pulling back the curtain and stepping out into full view of the other shoppers in here. The store assistant holds out her hand for my number again but also for the dress, probably presuming that I was only trying it on for fun and that there is no way I will actually be able to afford to buy it. But to her surprise, I only hand her the number, and I keep the dress for myself, smiling at her to let her know that it's a perfect fit, and I am now on my way to the checkout to pay for it.

As I make my way through the busy store, I'm tempted to peruse a few more options on the clothes rack but decide against it because while money isn't my biggest concern anymore, I still have to exercise some restraint. It would be fun to blow everything on dresses and leave this life looking like an absolute queen, but I do need to eat too, so I better save something for boring things like sustenance.

Joining the back of the long line at the checkout, I gaze at the other women queuing in front of me. They're all very different. Some tall, some short, some fat, some thin. Some looking nervous because they are overspending, others looking a little bored like they have just borrowed their rich husband's credit card again while he is at work. But I doubt any of them are dying like I am. I bet most of them are treating this like just another day at the shops, which I am slightly envious of but not as much as I thought I might be. That's because I can guarantee one thing that separates me from all these women.

I feel more alive right now than they ever have.

As the queue moves forward, I briefly consider picking up something from the long row of shelves filled with discounted goods which are always put here to tempt the queuing shoppers into making one last purchase before they reach the checkout. But there's nothing that catches my eye in particular, so I might as well save my money for something that does. But it's not long until something does catch my eye, and it's infinitely better than anything that I could have seen on the discount shelves.

It's the TV screen above the checkout clerk's head, set to play the news, presumably to give the people queuing something to do while they wait to part with various sums of money. Now, everybody in this queue is watching the screen just like me, as well as many other shoppers passing by in the area. That's because the newsflash is stating that an arrest has been made in the murder case that has shocked this part of the world and left several people fearing for their safety.

Andy's murder may no longer be the mystery that so many consider it to be. That's because there is now a suspect and the name scrolling across the bottom of the screen is a familiar one.

Claire King.

My ex-best friend.

Andy's ex-wife.

The woman I framed for his murder.

I hear the gossiping voices of the women around me, some of whom came together, some of whom are alone but feel the need to speculate about this with a complete stranger.

'I had a feeling it was his ex-wife,' says the old woman behind me, making me smile as I turn around and look at her. 'Hell hath no fury like a woman scorned,' she adds, and I nod my head because I couldn't agree more.

But I've never been one to engage in tittle-tattle, so I turn back around and face the checkout again, doing my best to remain impartial about all of this even though I am tempted to say that I used to know the suspect and even knew the victim as well. That would surely give the old woman some entertainment, as well as providing her with plenty to pass on to all the old girls at the bowls club she is probably a member of. She would also most likely want to know if I ever suspected Claire was capable of such a thing, of which I would have to say that I wasn't. No, I did not know that my best friend was capable of murdering her ex-husband.

It's unpredictable.

Terrible and unpredictable.

One thing that is predictable is that this long queue of shoppers eventually gets seen to, and I'm at the checkout before I know it, handing the dress over to the young man on the other side of the counter so he can remove the security tag and swipe the barcode. He does just that before telling me, rather shyly, that I now owe him, or rather his employer, the princely sum of £1000. But I don't bat an eyelid as I reach into my handbag and take out my purse before slotting my credit card into the machine and entering the pin.

The money is transferred electronically from my drained account into the bulging one belonging to this retail store, and by the time I remove the card and return it to my handbag, the dress is now officially mine to take and wear as I please. That is a good feeling, and I thank the man who made it all possible as I receive the shopping bag from him and turn to leave the checkout so that he can get on with serving the rest of the shoppers waiting behind me.

But before I leave the store, I turn back for one last look at the TV screen, and that's when I see her being taken from her house in handcuffs while surrounded by several police officers. Some savvy journalist had obviously managed to get to the scene in time to witness the arrest and has now sold footage of that dramatic moment to the highest bidder, giving me and the rest of the people in this town the opportunity to witness it for ourselves now. I'm glad of that too because how else would I have had the pleasure of seeing Claire being loaded into the back of a police car with a stunned expression on her face?

The poor woman will have no idea why she has been arrested for Andy's murder, but she will do soon enough. With her connection to the deceased, and more importantly, her motive for murder, the police are going to have plenty to talk to her about. But it will be the several strands of blonde hair that were discovered in the shower beside the dead body that will interest them the most. Those strands belong to her and were placed there by me after I took them from the coat she left at my house, placing her at the scene now and in the immediate vicinity of where the shocking crime took place. That coat has now been disposed of.

If only she hadn't left it at mine.

Claire may laugh off the suspicions that she could have done something as violent as this, as well as plead her innocence, but the police won't be laughing, and eventually, Claire will stop and take things seriously. Only then will she realise that she is going to go down for a long time.

By the time she gets out of prison, I will be dead.

But she won't be too far off the end of life herself by then either.

24

GRAHAM

There are plenty of ways you can get a shock. Sticking your finger in a plug socket. Putting a knife into a toaster when it's turned on. Or simply feeling the static from the seat when you get into your car. But these days, you can get just as much of a shock from turning on the television and watching the news. That's what I just got.

A shock, and a bloody big one at that.

Apparently, Claire King is now the prime suspect in the murder of her ex-husband, Andy.

Claire. The woman I embarked on an affair with. The woman I thought I loved once. And the woman who did her best to blow up my marriage after I spurned her and chose my wife instead.

At the time, I thought I'd been unlucky that Claire had decided to tell Alison everything, but watching the news now, maybe I was wrong. Maybe I should consider myself lucky because things could clearly have been much worse. Claire could have got revenge on me in a much more brutal way, just like she did to poor Andy.

I might be lucky to be alive.

But that concept is based on these news reports being true, and I'm not sure they are. Could Claire really have killed Andy? While it might seem like she had the motive after he cheated on her and gave her little option but to divorce him, I'm not sure that means she would have felt the need to go and butcher him to death in his new home. That just doesn't seem like something Claire could do because while she is many things, I seriously doubt she is a killer.

Then again, who knows? She could be a complete psycho, and the police wouldn't have taken her in unless they had real evidence to put alongside the motive.

There is no doubt that this is crazy news, and it's the kind that requires urgent alcohol intake to help process. That's why I find myself taking a cold beer from the fridge before returning to the TV and watching to see if there are any more updates on this shocking case. But there are none. Just that endless clip of footage being played over and over again on a loop, the one which shows Claire being taken from her home and into the back of a police car. It's the same home where I spent many a secretive hour behind my wife's back, although I didn't see much of the property other than the bedroom. But now that property is famous, being broadcast on TV screens all over town and probably the country, known for being the home of an alleged killer who mercilessly murdered her ex-husband to get revenge on his cheating ways.

I wonder if the house will become one of those places where local kids gather after school and gossip about the dangerous woman who used to live there as the property stands empty, struggling to be resold thanks to its connection to a grim past. It might even be the kind of place where strange types make a pilgrimage to and from other parts of the country, weirdly fascinated with the killer and the crime, and wishing to take a photo of the house where the infamous woman once lived. There may even be some budding entrepreneur in the area who tries to cash in on this crazy story and sell some form of merchandise that makes reference to this crime, a tawdry t-shirt perhaps that says something tacky about the incident but will no doubt appeal to some of the strange people who lurk in the dark corners of the internet.

But I don't care if kids gather outside the house or morbid types get titillated by the crime. What I care about is the truth and whether or not Claire really did this. If so, I was literally in bed with a killer. If not, she probably has one hell of a battle on her hands to prove her innocence and may not be lucky enough to do it.

I'm not sure which thought is scarier. That I was intimate with a murderer or that an innocent woman might end up behind bars for the next twenty-five years? That's probably why I decide not to think too much about either of them and just concentrate on drinking my beer as fast as I can instead.

It's only a couple of minutes later when I hear the key in the lock, and the front door opens. Alison is home from her trip into town. I wonder if she has seen the news.

I'm just about to grab the remote and turn the TV off because it might not be the best thing for her to come home and see when she enters the room and catches me before I have the chance. She notices my flustered face before she sees the news, but when she does, she drops her shopping bags in shock and puts her hands over her open mouth.

I pick up the remote, still intent on turning it off, but Alison stops me.

'Don't,' she says as she steps closer to the screen. 'Turn it up.'

I reluctantly do as I'm told and listen to the news reporter's voice run through the same spiel that I have heard him run through already before Alison got home. As my wife takes it all in for the first time, I slump onto the sofa and finish my beer, wishing I had more drinks to hand right now because these next few moments are no doubt going to be tricky for me to navigate successfully.

Having spent most of the time since I have been back in this house doing my best to get Alison to forget about Claire and our betrayals, now that woman's face is being broadcast into our home, and I imagine the sight of it is doing nothing to help my poor wife forget about what I did with her. I really wish I had been able to turn the TV off before she walked in because then I could have just asked her how her day was and hinted about how clean the house is now looking after I spent all morning going around it with a hoover and a feather duster. But that chance has gone now, and the tidy rooms around her are the last thing on Alison's radar as she continues to watch her ex-best-friend being marched into a police car by several burly officers in uniform who look as if they turned up at Claire's house ready for a fight.

'I think that's enough,' I eventually say when the footage loop begins for the fourth time, and the journalist starts going over the same facts that he just finished reading out.

Turning off the TV with the remote, I wonder if I will get any complaint from Alison, but she says nothing, instead joining me on the sofa where she sits in a state of quiet contemplation.

I want to say something, but I'm not sure what my next words should be. I'd love to not have to talk about Claire, but it seems like it would be almost laughable to talk about anything else after what we have just watched. Thankfully, it's my wife who ends up speaking first.

'She used to talk about all the different ways she wanted to kill him.'

'Excuse me?'

'Claire. After the divorce. When we used to meet up. She would talk about how she could kill him.'

'She did?'

'I thought she was just joking. I used to play along with her for fun and to make her feel better. I never thought she would actually act on it.'

While that is a worrying revelation, I am still harbouring doubts about whether or not Claire is really the person who killed Andy. But I perhaps rather wisely decide not to say that because sticking up for my mistress in front of my wife is surely the fastest way for me to end up sleeping on my office floor again. Instead, I just reach out and take Alison's hand, feeling glad when she doesn't pull away.

'You couldn't have known she was going to do this,' I tell her, doing my best to make her feel better in case she is worrying. 'Just because she talked about doing it, it doesn't mean you should have known it was going to happen.'

'I guess.'

'People talk about things like that all the time, I imagine. Killing their bosses. Killing annoying celebrities. Killing ex-partners. It doesn't mean any of them actually do it.'

‘Except Claire did.’

I hesitate because I’m surprised that Alison has already decided on Claire’s guilt. Then again, Claire is her least favourite person in the world right now, probably only just edging out me, so I can’t be too shocked that she has taken the side of the police.

I decide to say nothing more for fear of aggravating Alison and ending up out of the house. Much better to sit here in silence at home than being thrown out loudly again.

We both ended up sitting there for a while, hand in hand in silence, the black television screen in front of us almost teasing us to turn it back on so we could get another look at the murder suspect being taken to the police station. But we didn’t turn the TV back on. Neither of us wanted to.

We had seen enough, and we had both had enough bad news to last us a lifetime.

25

ALISON

For someone who has become used to people giving her bad news, it's rather pleasant to now be the one who gets to dish it out. That's why I'm almost enjoying this interaction with Dr Wilcox after I have just finished telling him that I do not wish to receive any further treatment for the disease that continues to spread inside me.

'It's my body. I can do what I like,' I say as the doctor frowns and eyes me with concern.

'That is correct, but you need to realise that with treatment, you will have the best part of a year left. But without it, I can't guarantee you will be here in four months.'

It's a sobering statement, but to me, it doesn't mean much because either way, I still end up with the same result. Death. Just one choice will delay it, while the other will speed it up.

It's hardly what I would consider having options.

'I've made my mind up. I don't want to spend what time I have left hooked up to a machine or throwing up into a toilet. I want to stay as active and healthy for as long as possible, and with all my own hair if I can help it.'

Dr Wilcox studies me, presumably to try and gauge if my thoughts are coming from a place of genuine honesty or if I am still somehow in denial about my illness and think that I can just ignore it and go on living until it leaves me alone again. But I remain calm, still and composed, and I guess that's enough for him to see that I have thought long and hard about this and have come to this considered conclusion.

He lets out a deep sigh before picking up the file on his desk and turning the page. I watch him jot something down, although I can't see what it is from here. It could be something important, or it could just be a tick box exercise to record that he has tried his best with me but cannot force me to have treatment if I decide not to. But he has nothing to worry about. I'm not going to sue him for medical negligence, nor is anybody in my family. I have made my decision in sound mind, and I have told all those people who are close to me what I wish to happen next. Of course, they weren't happy about it. My parents begged me to reconsider. My cousins cried and wished there was something they could do for me. And my husband even got angry and told me I was being selfish, just before I reminded him that he had started it when he went and slept with my best friend.

Despite all of their grievances, I am sticking to my decision. I am forgoing all treatment options, and I am leaving the cancer to run its natural course. Whether that means I have four months to live, twelve, or somewhere in between, so be it. I can't change the fact that this disease is going to kill me, but I can change how I choose to fight it, or rather, how I choose to let it take me.

I know there are plenty of people who consider my decision to be a foolish one, Dr Wilcox amongst them, but they are wrong. On the other hand, some people might look at it as brave. They might think that I am being bold and defiant in the face of such darkness and showing that every person with a life has the right to choose how it ends. But they would be wrong too. I'm not being foolish or brave.

I'm being sensible.

With the plans I have already set in motion, and the actions I still need to take, I can't afford to be wiped out by brutal bouts of chemotherapy, lying lifelessly on a bed or clinging to the side of a toilet as I heave and sweat. I need to be as fit and mobile as I can be for as long as I can be, and while I will inevitably decline, most likely rapidly, I am still well enough to go about my business for the foreseeable future. But after staying well enough to finish what I have started and complete my revenge on those who have wronged me, I need to be in a position where death will come fairly quickly for me then. That's because there is no guarantee that my plans will work, and I may end up getting caught and hauled off to the same police station that Claire is currently being interrogated in. If so, and the police can prove that I was the one who killed Andy, as well as committed the other acts that are yet to come, then I don't want to be around long enough to find out what they are going to do to me.

There are many negatives to a terminal diagnosis, but one of the positives is that the patient no longer has to worry about being sent to prison for life.

In these cases, life will be very, very short.

It's a win-win, in a weird way. I live long enough to do what I have to do but not so long as to face punishment if things go wrong and I get sent down. Of course, there is the possibility that I have my revenge and get away with it all, meaning it would be nice to have plenty of years left to savour the satisfaction that comes with the victory. But by then it will be too late, and I will succumb to my cancer quickly because I decided to forgo life-prolonging treatment now. But I can't have everything. There are risks whatever I decide to do, and no matter which path I choose, I end up in the same place.

The local funeral parlour.

With that in mind, I am satisfied I have come to a conclusion that fulfils all my objectives and reduces my risk to a minimum. I know I will die much quicker now, but there is a kind of freedom in that. It's amazing what you feel like you can do when you know you're going to be gone soon and won't be around to pick up the pieces or face the music. I feel liberated, like I can do anything, and it doesn't matter what the consequences are because, by the time they come around, I'll be pushing up daisies in the cemetery.

I imagine it's difficult to understand it if you aren't in the same boat, which is why my family, my husband and the doctor sitting opposite me have all had trouble doing so. I suppose to them, they cannot fathom why I wouldn't want an extra six months to live. But they also don't know what it is like to kill a man and get away with it, just as they don't know what it is like to do what I am planning next. They most likely see me as a silly, naïve or frightened woman who has been dealt a bad hand by the health gods and is now coming to the end of her life. But I don't see myself that way.

I see myself as somebody who has just enough time left to do everything I need to before I depart this life, and not a second too late.

'Are we finished here?' I ask the doctor as I continue to sit in silence in his office. 'I don't want to be rude, but I have rather a lot of things to be getting on with.'

Dr Wilcox stops writing and looks up from his notes, and I see the sadness in his eyes. He so desperately wants to help me, but he knows that he can't. Not completely anyway. Despite all his medical knowledge and experience, he knows this is one illness that is too far gone to be pulled back. With that in mind, he nods his head and sits back in his chair.

'I wish you all the very best. But don't hesitate to contact me if you change your mind.'

I thank him for his kind words before standing up and leaving his office, striding through the busy waiting room, which is filled with other women of a similar age to me, many of whom might be waiting to learn their own fates from the poor doctor who deals in deadly disease. It's hardly a job to send the spirits soaring, and I wonder how Dr Wilcox is able to switch off at the end of the day when he goes home and tries to relax. Can he lose himself in a football game or a comedy movie after spending twelve hours staring death in the face and issuing diagnoses like some kind of servant of the Grim Reaper himself?

Maybe he can. Maybe he has become skilled in the art of switching off and forgetting about his past, focusing instead on the present because that is all anyone can ever hope to control.

Maybe he has become as skilled at it as I have.

26

GRAHAM

It's been a while since I've been on the golf course. I tended to use this game as a way to clear my head and reduce stress, as well as it being a great way to get a break from responsibilities at home or in the workplace. But today, I'm not out on the fairways for those things. I'm out here because it's one place where I won't be bombarded by all the news reports and public gossiping about Claire and the fact she has now been charged with Andy's murder.

Seeing my ex-lover's face in the newspapers or being bandied about in the office kitchen has been difficult, but not just because I used to be so close to her. It's been difficult because I'm still not convinced that she is guilty. Despite what the police say and despite whatever evidence they must have on her that is making them confident enough to take her to trial, I just don't buy it.

Claire King is many things, but a killer she is not.

Unfortunately, my opinion counts for very little in most places, let alone a court of law, so it doesn't make much difference to her predicament whether I believe her pleas of innocence or not. All that matters now is whether the jury believes her, and that remains to be seen. The trial date has not yet been set, but I have a feeling they will rush it through the courts because of how much attention there is on it in the media. Everybody wants answers, most of all Andy's grieving family, so it won't help anybody to delay it. It certainly won't help Claire as she remains in custody, denied bail and made to sweat it out behind bars as the town waits to find out if she really is the dangerous killer that the police believe her to be.

Fortunately, there is no phone signal out here, nor are there any other people about, which means I can enjoy the next couple of hours free from having to hear, read or watch the news reports which tell me that the woman I once bedded is a mankiller.

Taking the putter from my bag, I step onto the pristine green and eye up the size of the task ahead of me. I need to get this ball in the hole from ten feet away while taking into account the slope of the green and the fact that I'm not exactly the best golf player in the world. This will be tricky, but not half as tricky as convincing Alison to let me back into our marital home.

As I stand over the ball and prepare to take my shot, I know I should be concentrating on the task at hand, but my mind can't help wandering back to my wife and how she has been behaving recently. She is still refusing all treatment options for her cancer, and while her symptoms haven't worsened yet, the ticking clock that seems to hover over her head seems to be getting louder by the day. I'm not sure how she is able to function with that fate following her around, but she seems to be managing it pretty well. She has been going to work and has helped train up some of the staff who are going to have to cope in her absence. She has been going out shopping and treating herself, even though it is a little concerning to see how much money she has been spending. But I can hardly tell her to stop enjoying herself when she won't be around this time next year. And she has been watching the news avidly since Claire was taken into custody, seemingly getting some enjoyment out of seeing her old friend trapped in her current predicament.

It's that last behaviour that is troubling me the most because while I can understand her being conscientious about her work, as well as her need to spend her money while she can, I can't see how she can be deriving any real pleasure from watching the news stories develop surrounding Andy's murder. Yet there she is, night after night, sitting in front of that TV waiting for the bulletins to begin as if she is sitting in a cinema waiting for the lights to go down so she can enjoy the latest blockbuster release. All she has been missing is the popcorn, but I bet she has thought about getting herself a bag for the next time.

I, on the other hand, have been trying my best to avoid the news, not wishing to hear all the reporting or speculating about the death of someone who was once a fairly close friend, as well as the incarceration of a woman who I knew deeply. But it's hard to get away from it completely when Alison has the damn TV set to the news channels whenever I walk into the living room to try and enjoy my evening.

As I continue to stand over the ball, trying to keep my body loose and my mind clear, I am struck by the vision of Alison sitting there on our sofa with a smirk on her face. I noticed the expression last night as we were sitting on the sofa together watching yet another news update. As the criminal expert on screen talked about what kind of sentence Andy's killer could expect to receive, I glanced at Alison out of the corner of my eye, and I noticed her lips were curled into a small smile. She was genuinely enjoying what she was watching and listening to, and I found that disturbing, even if she did have a reason for holding a vendetta against the accused.

So what if she hates Claire? That still shouldn't change the fact that Alison should be disgusted and shocked by what has happened to

Andy, as well as perhaps a little sceptical that such a slight woman as Claire could commit such a violent act of crime. Yet there seems no doubt in Alison's mind that Claire is guilty, as if she never used to be best friends with the woman and share coffee and cake with her on a weekly basis.

Alison keeps talking about how Claire liked to fantasise about killing Andy, as if that proves Claire must have acted on those fantasies now. But that doesn't sit right with me because first of all, why would somebody who planned to kill their ex-husband spend considerable time talking about how they would do it? Surely they would keep it a secret. To me, Claire's musings sound nothing more than the brief dalliances of imagination that they are. There is no substance to them. Just because somebody says they would like to hurt somebody, it doesn't actually mean they are going to do it.

I wanted to make this point with my wife, but not in an obvious way, so I asked her last night if she had ever fantasised about killing me after what I had done to her. She told me that she had and told me that it had proved to be an effective coping mechanism in the first few hours after the shock had subsided. While nobody wants to find out that someone else is imagining their death, I did say to Alison that it proved that Claire's fantasising might just have been as harmless as her own. But that didn't go down well because Alison quite rightly figured out that I was being supportive of Claire, so I stopped talking before I was told to start packing my bags again.

Now here I am with my golf clubs, which is the only bag I ever enjoy packing, but I'm not able to enjoy this once peaceful pastime of mine. That's because I can't escape the thought that has been nagging at me ever since it first popped into my head in the early hours of this morning.

It's the thought that Alison might have something to do with what has happened with Claire and Andy.

I know it seems ludicrous to even think it, and I had initially tried to laugh it off when I had first thought of it as I stared up at the ceiling in the spare bedroom while listening to the sound of the TV in Alison's bedroom next door. But the thought hadn't left me by the time the sun had come up and heralded a new day, and it still hasn't left me now out here, surrounded by luscious green grass and well-maintained bunkers of sand.

Did my wife have something to do with what happened to Andy?

Did she want Claire to be the suspect?

Is that why she is watching the news every night with a grin on her face?

It's little wonder that I end up missing the putt, sending my ball trickling harmlessly away from the hole and down the slope of the green to where it ends up almost back on the fairway again. I really am rubbish at golf, but that isn't bothering me today. What is bothering me is that I am good at one thing.

I am good at reading my wife.

And right now, I don't like what I am picking up.

27

ALISON

It's only April, but it's already been a hell of a year. In just a few short months, I have gone from thinking I would live to be a pensioner to learning that I probably wouldn't see Christmas. I've gone from thinking I had the perfect husband to learning that he had been cheating on me with my best friend. And I've gone from thinking that I could never be capable of such a thing as murder to knowing that I can not only do it, but I can get away with it too.

What a year. I can't wait to see what the rest of it brings.

It promises to be spectacular, and so it should be.

It will be my last one, after all.

But while there is still much to come, it's not going to be easy and not just because I have more dangerous acts to commit and get away with. It's because I'm starting to feel weaker by the day, and now I understand why Dr Wilcox was so disappointed when I told him I wouldn't be taking him up on his treatment options. It's because it's clear that I am not going to last long without them.

Those dresses I treated myself to on my shopping spree not so long ago now hang off me, no longer fitting as well as they did back in those changing rooms. My weight loss is not significant but substantial enough to let me know that it's not a product of any diet I'm on but rather is to do with the fact that my body is being ravaged internally. I regret not buying the dresses in smaller sizes in anticipation of this happening because then they wouldn't just be hanging uselessly in my wardrobe now, but never mind. I suppose I could try and find the receipts and take them back, but that would take time, and I have more important things to do.

Top of my to-do list today is a big one.

I need to return the call from the policeman that phoned me yesterday.

For most people, I imagine that finding out they had a voicemail on their phone from an officer of the law would be a worrying thing, but I had rather been hoping it would happen. That's because I needed the police to get in touch with me so I could tell them what I know about Claire and make it seem even more likely that she is the one who stabbed Andy to death in his shower.

It was vital that they contacted me first and not the other way around because if I had gone to them and told them that Claire liked to speculate about how she could kill Andy, Claire might quite rightly have smelled a rat and instructed her lawyers that I could be framing her for this crime. That's why I have waited for them to call me, which I knew they would get around to doing eventually because as one of her friends and close contacts around the time of Andy's death, at least if her mobile phone was anything to go by, then they would want to ask me a few questions. Nothing too serious, I imagine. Just enough to help them paint the picture of who Claire really is and, most importantly, what she might have been thinking around the time the murder took place.

Was she happy? Sad? Conflicted? Vengeful?

Who better to ask than a close friend of the accused?

I'm only too happy to help the police with their enquiries.

They should be here any minute, and I have just boiled the kettle in anticipation of their arrival.

It ends up being more like ten minutes before I hear the firm knock on the door, but that's fine by me. I am just grateful they were able to come to me instead of making me go down to the police station and have this conversation there. Not only would that have been a little more daunting for me, but it would have given me less chance to demonstrate how ill I am and how it has affected my home life. That's because I have made sure to leave out plenty of dirty dishes all over the kitchen counters, as well as making the living room as untidy as possible, all of which is supposed to show how little time I have had for housework since my shocking diagnosis. It's the diagnosis that I will make sure to slip into the conversation as early as possible, not only to get the officers to feel sorry for me but also not even consider the fact that they are actually sitting across from the real killer of Andy King.

'Hello,' I say as I open the front door before wrapping my dressing gown tightly around myself and squinting out into the sunlight, which is not at all bright to me, but I want to pretend like I've been sleeping in a dark room all day.

'Good afternoon. Alison Monroe?'

'That's right.'

'I'm PC Whittaker. This is PC Tenant. We called earlier to speak with you about Claire King?'

'Of course, come in,' I say, stepping back and allowing the uniformed men inside.

As I close the front door, I'm glad they have sent me males instead of females because that will make what I am about to tell them even easier. That's because a man would be shocked when I say that Claire talked about killing her cheating husband, whereas a woman would sympathise and possibly even relate to it.

I don't want to garner sympathy for Claire.

I want to garner disgust.

After offering the two men tea and pouring them a cup, we take our seats in the messy living room, where I waste no time explaining why the house is in the sorry state it is.

'I'm so sorry. You'll have to excuse the mess, but I haven't been well enough to keep on top of all the housework lately. I have cancer, you see, and there's not much they can do for me now.'

'Oh, I'm sorry to hear that,' PC Whittaker says, looking dreadfully upset, which is very endearing. PC Tenant, on the other hand, just looks awkward, and he says nothing, instead opting to keep his eyes fixed on the basket of washing I strategically placed in the corner earlier.

'That's okay. It's not your fault,' I reply, shaking my head. 'Just a terrible disease that sadly affects so many people. But would you believe I'm the first person in my family to have cancer? I suppose we've been fortunate in a way, although our luck has run out now.'

I purposefully brought the sombre mood in the room down even lower before taking a sip of my tea and pretending like I am sorry for doing so.

'I apologise. You didn't come here to hear about me and my woes. You want to talk about Claire, is that right?'

‘Yes, we were hoping you could tell us about your relationship with her if that’s okay?’

‘Of course. Claire and I were good friends. You know the kind who get together and gossip regularly. Putting the world to rights over a slice of cake and a good cup of tea.’

‘I see. You say you were good friends?’

‘Yes, that’s right.’

‘What happened?’

I pause because I know that giving up this information to them is risky but not as risky as withholding it.

‘Claire had an affair with my husband. Obviously, I didn’t care to see her again after that.’

Both police officers look shocked, and PC Tenant quickly averts his eyes from me and back to the washing basket again.

‘Oh, I’m sorry,’ PC Whittaker says, and I have now lost count of how many times the polite policeman has apologised to me since he walked through my door five minutes ago.

‘That’s okay. I’ve moved past it now. More important things to worry about,’ I say, making it obvious that I am referring to my ailing health.

‘When was the affair?’ PC Whittaker asks.

‘Within the last year. But I don’t know exact dates, sorry. I didn’t really ask.’

‘Of course.’

'How did you find out about it?' PC Tenant says, surprising me with his sudden query. I guess there is more to him than his awkward behaviour would suggest.

'It was actually Claire who told me about it,' I reply, now taking my turn to look meekly in the direction of the dirty washing, as if mentally recalling that dark day when my happy marriage came crashing down.

'She did?'

'Yes. She knocked on my front door and when I opened it, she told me that she had been sleeping with my husband.'

'Why would she do that?'

The questions are coming thick and fast from PC Tenant now, and I'm going to have to be on my game not to stumble over any of them and stick to my carefully rehearsed spiel.

'I believe it was because my husband wasn't going to leave me for her. I think she was angry about that and wanted to get back at him by telling me his secret.'

'Sorry, what's your husband's name?' PC Whittaker asks, interjecting before his suddenly eager colleague can fire any more queries towards me.

'Graham.'

I watch as the policeman jots that name down in his notebook, and I expect it will soon be my husband's turn to face these two men and their questions.

'So what happened then?' PC Tenant asks.

'Do you mean, did I forgive my husband?'

He nods.

'Yes, I did. I threw him out like any broken-hearted wife would do, I suppose. But with my diagnosis and the fact that I know I don't have time for petty emotions like bitterness or anger, I allowed him to come back.'

'That was very understanding of you.'

'Perhaps. Or maybe I'm just frightened of being alone in my last few months.'

I'm laying it on thick with the worries about my impending death, but I'm making my point, which is that I am just a dying woman and not the person who is really behind the murder that has got these officers working overtime.

'So did you speak to Claire after that day when she told you about the affair?'

I know why they are asking me that question in that way. They are seeing if I am telling the truth or if I am capable of lying, but I know they will have been through the accused's phone records by now, so I better make sure to be honest.

'Yes. I phoned her a few days later. I can't remember when exactly, but it was after I found out my cancer was terminal.'

'And why did you do that?'

'I don't know. It was silly of me. I think I wanted to make her feel bad for what she had done to me but also rub it in a little that my husband had chosen a dying woman over her.'

'And what did Claire say to that?'

'She was shocked about my illness. But I'm not sure how bad she really felt. It was hard to tell over the phone.'

'And did the two of you meet up or speak again after that phone call?'

I shake my head.

PC Whittaker closes his notebook, and I wonder if that means he is almost finished with me. But I can't let them go without telling them the thing I really want to get across.

'Do you really think Claire killed Andy?' I ask, doing my best to sound concerned.

I know there is no way they are going to come out and answer that honestly but I don't care about that. I'm just hoping they ask me the same thing in return.

'She has been charged, but it will go to trial,' PC Whittaker replies. 'In the meantime, we're just talking to anybody she might have been close to or in contact with around the time of Mr King's death to see if there's anything that could be relevant for the case.'

'I understand,' I say before glancing at PC Tenant in the hope that it will prompt him to ask me for my opinion on this case that has gripped the town.

'Based on what you know about Mrs King,' PC Tenant says, clearly going where I was hoping he would go. 'Do you think it is possible that she killed her ex-husband?'

I pretend to be a little shocked at the blunt question before taking a moment to compose an answer.

'I was obviously mortified when I saw that she had been arrested on the news,' I begin, shaking my head and wondering if I'm overplaying it before deciding that I'm not and carrying on. 'But then, I did think back to some of the things she used to say to me when we were friends.'

The officers glance at each other before PC Whittaker opens his notebook again.

'And what was that?' he asks me, his pen poised, ready to make a record.

'Well, you know Andy cheated on her, right?' I say, and the policemen nod, so I continue. 'So sometimes, when we would meet up after that, she would play this silly game where she would tell me about how she had fantasised about killing him that week. You know, nonsense stuff like chopping his willy off with a pair of hedge clippers or running him over when he came out of the pub.'

I see both men noticeably wince at the mention of what Claire used to talk about, and I suspect it has more to do with the hedge clipper part than the running over part.

'She used to say that?' PC Tenant asks when he has stopped fidgeting in his seat and imagining a crazy woman coming to chop his bits off with a garden tool.

'Yeah, but it was just a little game, really. Just a bit of fun to cheer herself up, I think. I mean, which woman wouldn't fantasise about doing those things to a husband who cheated on her?'

PC Whittaker writes something in his notepad while PC Tenant stares at me blankly before speaking again.

'Did you ever get the impression that she might have been serious about killing her ex-husband?' he asks me, and PC Whittaker stops writing to look up in time for my answer.

'Who, Claire? I don't think so,' I say, before purposefully pretending to have second thoughts. 'Well, I don't know now that this has happened. But at the time, no, of course I didn't think she would kill him.'

'What about mentioning stabbing him in the shower? Did she ever say that?'

I scratch my chin and do an impression of somebody trying to recall an old memory.

'I'm not sure,' I say, being purposefully vague. 'It's been a while, and my head is all over the place with my illness.'

‘Of course, we understand,’ PC Whittaker says before closing his notebook for the final time and letting me know that they have no further questions for me.

I’m pretty sure I have done a good job of putting plenty of doubts in the police officers’ minds, and as they stand up to leave, I allow myself a small smile of satisfaction at a job well done. By the time I have closed the door on them and heard their car moving away down the street, I am positively beaming.

28

GRAHAM

The only bad thing about playing a round of golf is that it has to end, and now this one is over. On the bright side, I'm currently making my way onto the "19th hole", which is the affectionate nickname for the pub that every self-respecting golfer frequents after they have finished on the fairways and have earned a little refreshment.

Ordering my pint with the lovely young lady behind the bar, I make several quips about the course and the weather, doing what I can to get a smile from her, and she is accommodating enough, although only because she is being paid to stand here and be friendly to the club members. Take us both out of this setting and put us somewhere else, and I doubt a nineteen-year-old woman like her would be listening to a man like me. As it is, she is employed to stand there and provide a little eye candy for the punters, so I might as well enjoy the interaction with her while I can. It won't be long until I'm going back home to Alison, who wouldn't smile at me these days even if she was being paid to.

Receiving the pint of bitter from the barmaid's dainty hands, I thank her and carry it over to one of the tables, deciding not to point out to her that she has made a mess of pouring it and that it shouldn't be as cloudy as it is. I don't want her to think I'm an arsehole, after all.

As I sink into my chair and take the weight off after an afternoon of hacking my way around the golf course that never seems to get any easier, I take a sip of my drink and watch the barmaid serving one of the other members. It's now his turn to try and get a smile out of her just to make himself feel better, and to be fair, he manages it, even getting a laugh from the young woman, which was more than I could ever hope to achieve.

Letting out a deep sigh, I reach into my pocket and take out my phone, turning it on after depriving myself of it for the last few hours while out on the greens. I've been glad of the break from the outside world, but I can't ignore it forever, and as my phone turns on, I notice the usual array of notifications coming through on the screen. Messages from friends. Notifications from the few social media channels I still use these days. And an update about the weather, even though I don't know why I bother getting these because it's always the same.

Grey. Windy. Average.

But then I see a notification that I don't get all too often flash up on my screen. It's telling me that I have a voicemail message from a missed call, so I click on it to give it a listen while I enjoy my poorly poured pint. But then I hear who it is from, and I choke on the frothy liquid, causing the barmaid to look in my direction and probably wonder what is wrong with me.

I give her a wave to let her know that I am alright, but that's only for show. Internally, I am all at sea, and that's because the voicemail is from a PC Whittaker, and he wants me to give him a call back to arrange a time when he can talk with me.

Realising that I have spilt several drops of my drink down my jumper, I brush them off while thinking about why this policeman would want to speak to me. The only thing I can think of is that Claire must have told them that she had been in a relationship with me, and now they want to speak to me because I would have been one of the last few people to be close to the murder suspect before Andy was found dead. Perhaps they just want me to corroborate something she has told them about their relationship or even just help get an idea of her state of mind over these last few months. But then another thought occurs to me, and it is a troubling one.

What if Claire, through sheer desperation, has used me in some kind of alibi which she is hoping will prove her innocence? Is she hoping that the feelings I once had for her still exist somewhere and that I can now help her get out of this mess? If so, I really wish she had found some way of letting me know because if she does need me to say something to the police, then it would help if I knew what it was.

But then I take another sip of my pint and decide that it can't be it. Claire won't be wanting me to lie for her and give a false alibi that gets her off the hook for Andy's murder. Why would she? She is most likely innocent and doesn't need me to get her out of this. The police probably just want to talk to everybody she was in close contact with recently and see if there were any clues as to what she might have been planning.

But there were not, and I will make sure to tell the police that.

I certainly won't be mentioning what Alison told me about Claire fantasising about killing her ex-husband. That would surely not go down well with the investigators if they found out about that.

I'm halfway through my pint when I pluck up the courage to call the number back and speak to PC Whittaker to set up the meeting. But he doesn't answer this time, and now it's my turn to leave a voicemail. But I don't mind that because if it delays me having to sit down with a policeman and recount my relationship with Claire for an extra day or two, then so be it.

As I finish my pint, I gaze at the pretty barmaid and wish I could have another drink, but I know it isn't worth the risk of being pulled over by the police on the way home and breathalysed. I know there have been a few members over the years here who have been caught out by a plucky policeman in these country lanes surrounding the club, punished for having one drink too many and losing their licence. The thought of a man needing his wife to drive him to this club every time he wants to play a round is a grim one because this is where men come to get away from their wives. With that in mind, I'll give the second pint a miss and call it a day, at least here anyway. I'll no doubt have a drink or two when I get home, especially if Alison is being frosty towards me.

I give the barmaid a smile and a wave as I stand up to leave, doing my best to look cool but probably not doing a very good job of it, before I walk out of the bar and out into the car park. I suspect it will be another week or so before I make it back here unless one of my friends unexpectedly asks me to come for a round, in which case I'll make the effort and return.

I reach my car, where my clubs are already stored safely away in the boot, and I climb in behind the wheel, ready to go home and see my wife. But before I can start the engine, I feel the vibration of my phone in my pocket and take it out to see a number I don't recognise calling me.

'Hello?'

'Hi. Is this Graham Monroe?'

'Yes.'

'It's PC Whittaker. I left a voicemail on your phone a short time ago, and I believe you just tried to call me back.'

I let out a sigh because I was hoping he wouldn't get back to me this quickly. I really hope he doesn't want to speak to me today.

'That's right. I'm sorry I missed you earlier. I was out on the golf course,' I tell him, hoping that by keeping things light, we won't have to get onto any heavy stuff when we do eventually speak in person.

'I'm envious. I haven't played a round in weeks. How was it out there?'

'The course was lovely, but my game was atrocious,' I jest, and I hear the chuckle of the officer at the other end of the line.

'Sounds familiar. Anyway, sorry to bother you, but I was hoping you might be free to talk. It's regarding Claire King.'

'Erm, sure,' I say, trying not to sound too aggrieved. 'When would you like to chat?'

'How about today?'

Damn. I might as well have had that second pint now because I'm going to end up face to face with a copper anyway.

Just my luck.

29

ALISON

I would have thought Graham would have been home by now after finishing his round of golf, but there is still no sign of him or his golf clubs in the hallway. Normally, I would be disappointed about him being late home, but these are not normal times. Ever since he cheated on me, I find myself going hours without even thinking about him. But today, I'm not enjoying his absence because I no longer love him as much as I used to. I'm enjoying it because I'm wondering if his late arrival home means the police have been in touch with him regarding Claire and their investigation into her alleged crime.

It's been a few hours since PC Whittaker and PC Tenant left my house, and I have spent most of that time putting the place back together again so that it doesn't look too much of a mess for when Graham gets back. I don't want him to know that I had purposely made the house look messy in preparing for a visit from the police so they could see how ill and run down I was. I want him to find out about my conversation with the officers as late as possible, preferably when he is being interviewed by them himself. I'm sure it will come as a surprise for him to hear that the two policemen have already spoken to me about my relationship with Claire, and particularly that they know all about the affair and the love triangle of sorts that existed between the three of us. It will also come as a surprise if he hears that I told them about what Claire used to tell me about Andy, namely all the ways she would like to kill him.

I'm not sure how Graham will handle being spoken to by the police about the woman he used to be intimately involved with, but I have to imagine it will be awkward for him, to say the least. But so what? He can suck it up, just like I had to when I found out he was cheating on me.

I take off the towel that I used to dry myself after getting out of the shower and go to leave the bathroom, but as I do, I catch a glimpse of myself in the mirror, and it's a little shocking to see how skinny I have become now. There is no doubt about it; my body is wasting away, and I'd be surprised if I make it to the end of summer, never mind Christmas. But thankfully, I am not in much pain yet, nor am I fatigued enough to prevent me from doing what I need to do so I will make the most of my mobility while I still have it. I seriously doubt I would be this fit and agile if I had opted for chemo instead of letting my disease run its natural course.

I'd either be at the hospital now or curled up on my mattress in the bedroom, writhing in agony and trying to control another bout of nausea.

I feel like I made the right choice.

Less time to live.

But better days to enjoy.

Strolling naked into the bedroom, I think about how amusing it would be if the window cleaner was standing on his ladder outside my bedroom window and got an eyeful of me leaving the bathroom. He would probably take a tumble, and I would get a good giggle at him as he went. Alas, there is no sign of any window cleaner outside, so I am free to get dressed in privacy, my impromptu exhibitionist streak going to waste for today, at least.

Opening my wardrobe, I peruse my options, which are growing more and more limited by the day thanks to my weight loss. But I'm determined to make this a special evening, and that calls for a special dress, so I take out the black number on the second rack and hold it up to my naked body. It won't look perfect, but it will do.

It'll be enough to distract Graham, and that's all I need.

I put on some of my finest lingerie first, wondering how many years it has been since these garments saw the light of day before slipping into my dress and easily managing to zip it up myself.

Long gone are the days when I would have to do battle with the zipper. Now, it goes up and down over my skinny frame so easily that it's almost as if I'm not even here.

With my outfit taken care of, I waste little time in bringing my face and hair up to speed, using my best makeup to revive my pale and slightly gaunt face and using curlers to bring a little life to my long, dark locks. This is another reason why I feel like I made the right decision to forgo chemo. My hair is my best asset, and I could never do anything to risk it, not even for the sake of an extra few months.

Looking good, I leave the bedroom and head downstairs, my bare feet padding over the carpet while I carry a pair of black heels in my hand. I put them on my feet as soon as I reach the bottom and then head into the kitchen to make a start on dinner. Tonight, I am cooking a three-course meal so tasty and sumptuous that it will cause Graham to salivate as soon as he hears all about it. But I can make a good start on it before he gets in, so that's what I do, turning on the oven, filling a couple of pans with water and taking out a sharp knife to chop all the vegetables that I need.

Singing away to myself as I slice an onion, I realise I haven't felt this happy in a long time. It's ridiculous, but it has taken a deadly diagnosis and the revelation of my husband's adultery to make me feel alive. But now that I feel this way, I can honestly say that I have never felt better. Maybe I'm deluded or in some state of shock that is going to wear off soon, and then my real emotions will hit me like a tsunami out of the blue. Or maybe not. I don't know. Dying of a terminal illness is not exactly something you can get practise for. Either you're lucky enough for it to never happen, or it comes for you all of a sudden. It has got me, and all I can do is deal with it in my own unique way. Fortunately, that way seems to be working out well for me so far.

I'm in such a groove with the onion chopping that I realise I've ended up doing too much and better throw some away, otherwise this meal will be overwhelmed by all the excess ingredients, and Graham and I will be stinking the place out with our bad breath. Scraping half of the onion into the pan and the other half into the bin because there's little point in saving it for another day, I get to work on the plump red pepper that looks juicy enough to take a bite out of.

As the knife slices effortlessly through the brightly coloured fruit, I think about how this object really is a wonderful invention. All this power and precision contained within such a small tool, its user getting to wield it as they wish simply by taking hold of the handle and making it move. I know most people just use knives for preparing meals, but that is such a waste of this item's potency. Blades like these deserve to cut through so much more than just fruit and veg. They deserve to run along the tip of a person's skin, the surface that offers a fine line between life and death and the option between no blood or lots of it.

I stop chopping for a moment and put my finger on the edge of the knife, pressing it against my skin harder and harder until it suddenly slips past it, and I let out a gasp as I feel the cutting pain in my hand.

Dropping the knife, I look down at my finger, and at first, it seems like I have gotten away with it until I see the small red river begin to form along the centre of my digit. Seconds later and the blood is plentiful, causing me to have to go over to the sink and run my finger under the tap to help wash it all away. Five minutes later and the blood is still flowing out though, so I guess I'll need to find a plaster to cover my wound now.

But before I do, I think about how there will soon be so much blood in this house that not all the plasters in the world could cover up and heal it all.

I got first-hand experience of what it looks like when a knife enters the human body when I killed Andy in his shower.

Tonight, I will get to see that same thing again.

I cannot wait for my husband to come home for dinner.

30

GRAHAM

I definitely should have had that second pint. At least then, I might have been slightly more relaxed during my conversation with PC Whittaker and his colleague, PC Tenant. As it was, I found myself feeling a little nervous as I sat across from the two men in the police station.

I had hoped to hold the conversation somewhere more informal, but my suggestions for places to talk were rejected based on time constraints. In the end, it seemed easier if I just offered to go to the station and get it over with. I didn't want this hanging over my head for another day or two, and I expected it to be a quick interaction anyway, so I left the golf club and made the six-mile drive to the station, spending most of the journey wondering what the officers' questions were going to entail.

How close were you to Claire?

Was she ever violent towards you?

Do you think she might be a killer?

It turns out that I had been asked all those questions, although not quite so bluntly, but I answered them all as honestly as I could. I told the two officers that I was close to Claire for a while, admitting the affair that I was guessing they already knew about. I also told them that in all that time, Claire was never violent towards me and that no, in my honest opinion, I didn't think she was a killer. But of course, I admitted that I could be wrong.

I had rather hoped that the questions would start to dry up from there, but then the conversation had taken a rather unexpected turn when the two PCs stopped talking about Claire and started talking about my wife instead.

'Tell us about Alison,' had been the exact words out of PC Tenant's mouth about twenty minutes into our conversation.

'What do you want to know?' I had replied, my mind racing as to why they had veered into this line of questioning.

'How is she doing?'

'Have you spoken to her?'

'Yes. But we would like you to tell us.'

I'd been concerned by the admission that the officers had already spoken to my wife because that gave me little doubt that Alison would have mentioned Claire's tendency to imagine killing Andy. Anything to send her love rival deeper into trouble. But the policemen weren't asking me to corroborate this part of my wife's statement.

Instead, they were just asking me about her, full stop.

That had been a little disconcerting, but I'd done as they had asked, telling them about her illness and how she had refused treatment, unsure why they were so interested but telling them as much as I could so that it didn't seem like I was being purposefully vague.

'I imagine things have been very difficult,' PC Tenant had said just after that, but the way he said it made me think there was more behind that statement than just a simple expression of sympathy.

'What do you mean?'

'Well, Alison has found out she has cancer and that you were having an affair, both in a very short time span. That would be difficult for anybody?'

I had to agree.

'How has your home life been recently?

'It's been okay.'

The two officers had glanced at each other at that point, and I hadn't been sure why.

'No offence, but it didn't look that way when we visited your house.'

'How do you mean?'

'It looked like your wife was struggling to keep on top of things. Like the housework, for example.'

I think I had frowned then because that had been an unexpected thing to hear. That's because as much as Alison had struggled recently, she had never let her standards slip at home. The house was always tidy, annoyingly so sometimes because it could feel like I was walking around a museum where I was afraid to touch anything or leave it out of its place. But these officers seem to think that our home was rather unkempt. If it was, then my wife must have purposefully made it look that way. But why?

Deciding that it was too risky to disagree with them, I had simply nodded and told them that housework was not exactly top of our list of priorities right now. At least that way, I didn't have to make them wonder why Alison had deliberately messed the house up just for their arrival. But I would like to know the answer to that myself at some point.

'How do you think your wife feels about Claire King?' PC Whittaker had asked me after that, and I had fumbled around for an answer that I thought might be the most suitable one.

'Well, they're not friendly anymore, if that's what you mean. But that's to be expected, I suppose.'

'Of course.'

PC Tenant's sudden agreeable nature had caught me by surprise, and the longer the conversation had gone on, the harder I had found it to get a good grasp on these two officers. They weren't playing good cop, bad cop. They were both simultaneously switching from being the aggressor in the questioning to being on my side and making me feel like I had nothing to worry about.

So why was I worried?

'Did Alison ever talk about wanting to get revenge on Claire for the affair?'

The question from PC Whittaker had come out of nowhere, but I had shaken my head and answered in the negative, several times in fact.

'No. Definitely not. She's not that kind of person,' I had said, my head going from side to side as if I was trying to convince myself as much as them.

'I wouldn't have blamed her if she had,' PC Tenant had added then. 'I imagine plenty of people who get cheated on spend at least a little time dreaming of revenge.'

That had been the moment when I knew for sure that Alison had told these officers about Claire's fantasies of killing Andy.

'I guess,' I had mumbled, growing more uncomfortable by the minute.

Then I had been asked the question I presume they had been waiting to ask me ever since they called to speak to me.

'Did Claire ever talk with you about getting her own back on Andy when he cheated on her?'

I had taken my time to answer that question, knowing that to answer too quickly could look bad either way. Either I could have said yes, and it would have really added to the suspicion on Claire now, or I could have said no, but the officers might have thought I was lying considering they already knew from Alison that Claire liked to imagine Andy's murder.

In the end, I had just told them what I could, which was something in between.

'She never said anything like that to me. But my wife told me that Claire would sometimes say those things when they were having coffee together.'

That had been about as honest an answer as I could have given, and I had felt good about it, right up until PC Whittaker had spoken again.

'Claire maintains her innocence and insists she has been framed for Andy's murder,' the officer had said while leaning back in his seat and folding his arms. 'When she was pushed to give the name of anybody whom she thought could be framing her, she gave us only one name. It was your wife's.'

'What?'

'Does that concern you?'

'Well, yes. Of course.'

'Do you think Alison might have been involved in Andy King's murder?'

'No! Do you?'

There had been a tense pause in the conversation then, and I had waited for one of the officers to give me an answer, wondering if they already had my wife in custody somewhere and this was all just a sneaky way to try and find out if I had been conspiring with her. But finally, one of the men had spoken again.

'No. We don't. We think Claire is just desperate and is telling us anything she can to get out of this. But we have to check these things. I hope you understand.'

The answer had been a simple one from PC Tenant, but it hadn't made me feel much better. That's because then, I had no longer been worried about whether or not they thought I was telling them the truth. Instead, I had been more concerned about if they were telling me the truth themselves.

Shortly after that, the two officers had told me that they had no more questions and that I could go home, which had been a relief and I had got up out of my chair quickly to head for the door. But before I had been able to open it, PC Whittaker had spoken again, and it was the words he had said then that were still rattling around in my head now, half an hour later as I sit outside my home and prepare to go inside to see my wife.

‘Good luck with all the housework.’

I had smiled at the man as I had left the room, but it had been a false expression and not one that reflected my mood at the time. The reference to my untidy house again had me troubled for two reasons. One, because I knew that my house was never untidy. And two, it seemed like the officers suspected that too, which must have meant they had their doubts about the way Alison had presented herself to them earlier.

But what does that mean? Do they think Alison might have been lying to them? If so, why? I know my wife would have been happy to tell them anything that might have incriminated Claire further in Andy’s murder, but I thought that was only because she hated the woman and would have been happy to see her suffer. But what if there was another reason why Alison had told them about Claire’s fantasies? What if it wasn’t from a place of bitterness? What if it was because Alison was covering up something she had done instead?

What if Alison was the one who killed Andy?

I should go inside my house because I’ve been sitting in my car on the driveway for long enough. But I feel like I don’t want to get out.

For some strange reason, I feel nervous about going inside and seeing my wife.

31

ALISON

The table is set, and the food is almost ready. All that's missing now is my husband.

I check my phone again to see if he has been in contact, but there is still no word, so I'm just about to go to the window and see if there is any sign of him arriving on the street outside when I hear the front door opening.

Quickly running my fingers through my hair and smoothing out any wrinkles in my loosely hanging dress, I walk into the hallway with a smile on my face.

'Hi. There you are. I was wondering where you had got to.'

Graham looks tired, but he soon perks up when he sees how I am looking.

'Sorry, I got held up at the golf club.'

'I thought you might have done. I hope you didn't have too much to drink.'

I walk over and give him a kiss on the cheek while also trying to detect the smell of beer on his breath. If there is a scent, it's only a mild one. He hasn't been drinking that much.

'No, of course not,' he says to me, accepting the kiss before closing the door behind himself. 'You look nice.'

'I thought I'd make an effort and wear something a little different. You like it?'

Graham nods, and if he does notice that the dress doesn't fit me well anymore, he doesn't comment on it, which is sweet of him.

'I've made dinner too,' I say, leading him towards the kitchen as soon as he has put his golf clubs down.

'I thought something smelt good.'

'It's a three-course Mexican,' I tell him as we enter the kitchen and take in the sights and smells of all my hard work this afternoon. 'Your favourite.'

'Wow, thanks,' Graham replies, and I see him hungrily eyeing up the bowl of nachos that have just come out of the oven.

'How about you go and quickly get changed while I dish up?

'Okay. Are you sure? I don't want you to overdo it?'

'I'm fine. Really.'

I smile at my husband so that he knows he is okay to leave the kitchen to go upstairs and change out of his unattractive golfing attire. While he does, I get to work on serving up the food. Alongside the nachos, there are chicken fajitas, beef tacos and even a few empanadas, which are more Spanish than Mexican, but we have always added them onto our Mexican nights in the past. This kind of meal for us is more than just a chance to gorge ourselves on some delicious cuisine. It is also a chance for the two of us to reminisce about the holiday we had in Mexico a couple of years ago. Those two weeks we spent visiting Cancun and Acapulco were probably the happiest two weeks of our marriage, and while we couldn't ever hope to recreate the sunny skies and sandy beaches once we had returned home, we could do our best to recreate the types of food we savoured while we were out there.

We usually have a Mexican feast at least once a month and spend the meal talking about that lovely trip we took. But it's been a while since we did that, for obvious reasons, but tonight it feels time to do it again. I'm ready to go back mentally to a time when I had my health and my happy marriage, before I got sick and he cheated, and everything seemed to go wrong so fast. I'd give anything to go back two years and be in Mexico again now, walking hand in hand with Graham on one of those beaches, but no one can go back.

We can only go forward.

As I hear my husband's footsteps in the bedroom above me, I plate up the tacos and place them in the centre of the table before returning to the counter to dish up the fajitas. There's enough food here for twelve people, never mind two, but I'm sure we'll manage. Graham has never struggled to eat more than his fair share of this cuisine, and while I would usually be a little more cautious about consuming so many calories, that's not something that I'm bothered about anymore. I could probably eat all of this and still struggle to put on weight now, which is one positive, I suppose. I am trying my best to look on the bright side of things.

With the food ready to go, the drinks are next, and I have picked out a special bottle of red wine for this occasion. It's one that I know Graham has had stored away at the back of the kitchen cupboard for a long time in anticipation of a special event, and while he might not have had an evening like tonight in mind, I think it is perfect. After all, it's not every day you can drink to the death of a marriage.

Uncorking the bottle and pouring two generous measures into our best wine glasses, I place the drinks on the table beside all the food, and now everything is almost ready. Everything except the knife, which I need to move from the kitchen counter to the table so that it is easier to use when I need it later.

The sound of Graham's footsteps coming down the stairs tells me that I am out of time in making this meal look as perfect as possible. This is as good as it is going to get, and I think I've done a sufficient job.

The food. The wine. The knife.

They are all going to be enjoyed in their own special way.

'This looks great.'

I turn around to see Graham standing in the kitchen doorway, looking smart in his dark blue shirt and black trousers. He has even added a little gel to his hair which he doesn't always do, at least not for me anyway. I wonder how much of an effort he made for Claire when they were meeting up for their secretive rendezvous, but it doesn't really matter. What does matter is that he is making the effort for me tonight and not her, so I guess that could count as me having the last laugh.

But I'm not laughing yet. There is still some work to be done before I really do end up coming out as the winner in this situation.

'Tuck in while it's warm,' I say, taking a seat and putting one of the napkins onto my lap.

Graham eases himself into the chair opposite me, and we are only separated now by the vast portions of food that sit on the table between us.

'What do you fancy first?' I ask him as I pick up the large knife and prepare to use it on dishing up some of the delicious treats on offer.

‘I think I’ll start with a fajita,’ he says, and I serve him quickly, aware of how hungry he must be after being out of the house for such a long time.

‘Which wine did you pour?’ he asks me as he picks up his glass and holds it below his nostrils to get a whiff of the scent.

‘The Zinfandel. I read it goes well with Mexican.’

Graham looks only slightly perturbed that I cracked open the bottle he has been saving for something else before he takes a sip and gives a nod of approval.

‘What are we celebrating?’ he asks me just before we start to eat.

‘Life,’ I say, reaching out across the table for his hand.

He reluctantly takes it, seeming a little awkward around me, but I don’t care. If he thinks things are awkward now, he should wait and see what I have in store for him after the meal.

‘To life,’ he says, his hand holding mine while his other goes back for his wine glass again.

‘To life,’ I repeat, picking up my own glass and clinking it against his. ‘To all those who have it and to all those who have lost it.’

Then I drink, leaving Graham to wonder what the hell I just meant by that.

I take my hand back and pick up my knife and fork, ready to get on with things.

‘Enjoy,’ I say before cutting into the bulky fajita on my plate.

As we tuck into the first part of our massive meal, I glance up at my husband and notice that he looks a little on edge. I’m not sure what it could be, but there is definitely something on his mind, and I will have to coax it out of him before the meal is over. But there’s no rush yet. We can just enjoy dinner for now.

The last dinner we will ever share together as a married couple.

32

GRAHAM

The food is good. The wine too. But the company?

I'm still not so sure about that.

I could put this impromptu dinner down to the fact that Alison knows time is running out for her, so she wants to make the most of the opportunity to do things like this. I could also put it down to her perhaps genuinely forgiving me for what I did with Claire and looking to make our last few months together as painless as possible. But I feel like that is too simplistic and not at all realistic. I don't think Alison has done this just because she wants a nice meal before she dies, and I certainly don't believe that she has forgiven me for cheating on her with her best friend.

So then what is this dinner really about?

I'm yet to find out because so far, Alison has spent most of it talking about the holiday to Mexico we had two years ago, which is pleasant enough, but isn't putting me at ease because I feel like something is coming. Something much bigger and more important than simply reminiscing about the past.

I take another large glug of wine and pray for its calming effects to kick in quicker so that I might be able to sufficiently relax and enjoy this awkward meal a little more. But so far, that hasn't happened, and I'm still on edge, caused no doubt by my conversation with the two police officers before I came home tonight.

I don't know whether they were just speaking to me as a formality because Alison had mentioned Claire and I, or whether they genuinely think that my wife might have something to do with Andy's murder like Claire seems to think. But if it's the latter, then why haven't they taken her in for formal questioning or even arrested her on suspicion? There must be no evidence and no reason for them to suspect her other than Claire's words, which could be attributed to her being desperate and willing to say anything just to get out of her predicament. But there was more than enough in the words of PC's Whittaker and Tenant to make me doubt my wife, and it's time I started to try and get a few answers, starting with the mysterious case of the untidy house.

'I hope you haven't been overdoing it on the housework,' I say to Alison in between mouthfuls of beef taco. 'You should be resting now. Leave it to me.'

'If I left it to you, then the place would be a bombsite,' Alison says with a chuckle before going for a second helping of empanadas.

I think about how the policemen told me the house did look like a bombsite when they visited here earlier and wonder why that was the case. But there's only one way to find out.

'Did the police speak with you about Andy's murder?' I ask, trying my best to make the question sound as casual as I can.

Alison stops eating for a moment, and I wonder how much I should read into that.

'Did they speak to you?' she asks me in return, and I know that answering a question with another question is never a good sign.

'Yes. This afternoon after I had finished at the golf course.'

I watch carefully to see if Alison seems surprised by that, but I can't tell. It's funny because I spent so much time wondering if she could read my behaviours when I was lying about where I'd been and who I'd been with, but now I'm the one trying to read her to see if she is being honest.

'Yeah. They spoke to me too,' she admits before taking another bite of her food.

'What did they ask you?'

'They just wanted to know about my relationship with Claire.'

'And what did you tell them?'

‘I told them about the affair if that’s what you mean.’

My wife’s reply is cutting, and I wonder if she said it as a reminder to me that I shouldn’t keep probing her if I want this meal to stay as quiet and as peaceful as it has been so far. But if so, I’m not going to give up that easily.

‘Did you tell them that Claire used to talk about killing Andy?’

‘I did mention it, yes.’

‘Why?’

‘Because I thought it was relevant. She did kill him, after all.’

My wife is certain of Claire’s guilt, but from what I gathered when I spoke to the police earlier, they are not.

‘Did you tell them that too?’ she asks me, possibly testing me to see if I still have any allegiance to my former lover and might have withheld damaging information that could reduce her chances of getting a “not guilty” verdict in the upcoming trial.

‘I did mention it,’ I admit.

‘Anything else?’

‘Not really. But the policemen did say something that had me a little confused.’

‘Which was?’

‘They said the house was very untidy when they visited here to speak to you. That sounded strange to me because it wasn't untidy when I left, and it wasn't untidy when I came home. So what happened in between?'

I pick up my wine glass while keeping my eyes on Alison, waiting for her answer.

'I wouldn't call it untidy. But I had got some washing out and was also cleaning the kitchen when they called around, so I guess that's what they mean.'

'So you didn't make it look messy on purpose?'

'Why would I do that?'

'I don't know. Maybe you wanted them to think you were struggling.'

'I am struggling.'

Alison's admission is a blunt one and catches me off guard a little.

'I'm dying, Graham. Just because I've put on a pretty dress and cooked a meal, don't think I have forgotten that.'

'I know, that's not what I meant.'

'Then what did you mean?'

I can hardly answer that honestly because to do so would be to reveal that both me and the police have some concerns about who really killed Andy King.

'I don't know.'

'I think you do.'

Our eyes are locked together as we have stopped eating now and sit in our chairs, trying to figure out what the other one is thinking. Am I reading too much into this? Is Alison really just trying to do something nice here? Or does she have secrets to hide, secrets that are far worse than anything I have ever kept from her?

'Do you remember what we did on this table not too long ago?' Alison asks me, surprising me with the change of direction in the conversation.

I think back to the time when we made love on this table. It was the day when I found out she was dying.

'Of course,' I say.

'Why do you think we did that?'

'I don't know. Shock. Passion. Grief, maybe. A mixture of emotions, I guess.'

Alison nods her head, but she doesn't seem convinced.

'For you, perhaps. But that wasn't why I did it.'

'Why did you?'

'I did it because I was full of adrenaline.'

'From what?'

Alison pauses before she answers my question.

'What do you think?' she finally asks.

I have no idea, and my expression must tell her that.

'Have a good think,' she says. 'Go back to that night. What else do you know happened on that evening that you didn't know at the time?'

I'm puzzled.

'What do you mean?'

'Think about it.'

I do as I'm told, trying to recall that night and anything else that might stick in the memory from it. But I can't remember much else, certainly not anything significant.

'I don't know,' I admit when I've had enough playing of this game.

'It was the night that Andy was killed,' she says coldly. 'They found his body the next day.'

I stare at my wife as I realise what she is getting at.

'What do you mean?' I ask her.

'What do you think I mean?'

'You killed Andy?'

'That would certainly explain why I was so full of adrenaline, wouldn't it?'

I don't know what to say or do. If she did kill him, then why the hell is she telling me?

'You killed him?'

Alison picks up her wine glass and takes a long sip. It's only when she puts it down again that she gives me her answer, and it comes in the form of a slow nod.

'Oh my god! Why the hell would you do that?' I cry, pushing back from the table and getting up from my chair as if I need to put some more distance between the two of us now.

'Why do you think?' Alison asks me, remaining still.

'I have no idea!' I cry, shaking my head.

'Oh, come on. I'm sure you can think of a good reason.'

I stare at my wife, almost in disbelief that a woman this calm and composed could have just admitted to the brutal murder of a man we both used to call a friend.

'You wanted to frame Claire,' I say, realising the horror of the truth.

Alison gives me a smile as she picks up her wine glass again.

'Correct,' she says before taking a satisfying sip.

33

ALISON

I've told my husband about what I did to Andy and why I did it. As I expected, he is no longer enjoying the meal. Instead, he is standing with his back against the edge of the kitchen counter as if he is afraid to get any closer to me.

He's afraid of me.

And so he should be.

'How could you do it?' he asks me as I continue to enjoy the lovely bottle of red that is just perfect for an occasion as momentous as this one.

'You mean, how could I kill a man?' I reply, returning my empty glass to the table. 'It's surprisingly easy, or at least it is if you have sufficient motivation.'

'You're crazy.'

'No. I'm dying. There is a difference.'

'What? So you think that just gives you the right to do whatever the hell you want?'

'I don't know. Maybe. I do know it is extremely liberating to know that I won't have to worry about being around long enough to suffer any consequences if I get caught.'

Graham looks at me with disdain, but I'm enjoying this because it's his turn to be shocked, disgusted and destroyed. This is exactly how I felt when I found out what he had been doing behind my back. Okay, so he hadn't killed anybody, but he had killed our marriage, and to me, that was just as bad.

'You're lying,' he says, refusing to believe it. 'You couldn't have done this.'

'The murder weapon is hidden in our spare bedroom, and there is a note of confession with it.'

That makes him believe me.

'You're serious?'

The expression on my face lets him know that I am.

'You can't let Claire go down for something you did,' he says, shaking his head. 'It's not right.'

'I think she gave up the concept of what's right and wrong when she slept with my husband, don't you?'

'That doesn't mean she deserves to spend the rest of her life in prison!'

'I disagree. She deserves to be punished, and that punishment should be decided by the person she wronged. That is me, and this is what I have decided.'

'I can't believe this,' Graham says, and he goes to leave the room.

'Where are you going?'

‘I’m calling the police.’

‘I wouldn’t do that if I were you.’

He stops in the doorway with his back still turned to me. That gives me the opportunity to reach out and pick up the knife from the table and discreetly place it in my lap should I need to use it in a moment or two.

‘Why?’ he asks me as he turns around and looks at me.

‘Because if you try and breathe one word of this to the police, then you will end up just like Andy.’

Graham’s eyes go wide as he registers what I have just said.

‘You’d kill me?’

‘If I havc to, yes.’

‘You’re a psycho.’

I shake my head.

‘No, I’m just a woman whose husband betrayed her. You can’t possibly understand how I feel. But Claire can. She knows exactly how this feels because Andy did the same thing to her. That’s why it’s even worse that she would willingly bring these feelings to somebody else. That is why she is the one in the frame for murder now and not you.’

‘So what? We’re just supposed to sit by and watch her go down for a crime she didn’t commit.’

‘Exactly.’

I shrug my shoulders as if it is as easy as that, although I know it isn't. I won't be sitting around watching anything. I have better plans than that.

'I can't do it,' Graham says, still maintaining a safe distance between us as he remains by the door. 'I can't let you get away with this.'

'I thought you loved me. I thought you wanted me over Claire.'

'That was before I knew you killed Andy!'

'That shouldn't change anything. Either you love me, or you don't.'

'Don't be ridiculous.'

I'm enjoying seeing Graham get so wound up, and I imagine his mind is a jumble of all sorts of thoughts and feelings. Anger. Guilt. Confusion. Shock. *And fear.*

He still looks absolutely petrified of me, and that's even before he knows about the knife I have hidden from view.

'What do you want from me?' he asks, suddenly looking as drained as I did before I put on my makeup and did my hair.

'I want you to prove that you really choose me over her,' I say, smiling at him.

'What do you mean?'

'If you really love me, then you won't tell anybody about this, and I will get away with it. If you still love her, then you will want her to be free, and that would be most disappointing.'

'It has nothing to do with love! This is about a woman's freedom. She is going to lose the rest of her life because of something you did!'

'And I'm going to lose the rest of my life because of sheer bad luck! Life isn't fair. Get over it!'

I didn't mean to raise my voice as loudly as I just did then, but I was overcome with raw emotion, and I guess there is still an anger that burns around the sense of injustice that my terminal diagnosis has given me. Fortunately, we are in a detached house, so I don't have to worry about any neighbours overhearing us. They would be getting quite the show if thcy could.

Graham still seems unsure about whether to take his chances by leaving the kitchen or re-joining me back at the table, so I decide to make things easier for him.

I decide to show him the knife.

Picking it up from my lap, I hold it out towards him, the tip of the blade pointed in his direction, as if it has him in its sharp sights, even from all the way over here.

'What are you doing with that?' he asks me nervously.

'I'm showing you the last thing that Andy saw just before he died.'

'Why?'

'Because I can.'

'So you think that by threatening to stab me, you can make me choose you over Claire's freedom? That hardly seems sensible. I could just be doing it to save my life. It wouldn't prove that I love you.'

'You're right, it wouldn't,' I say, nodding my head while keeping the blade in mid-air. 'But it's one way of making sure that bitch stays where she belongs.'

'But she doesn't belong there, does she? She didn't kill Andy. You did.'

'How else would you suggest I get my own back on her?' I ask him, momentarily putting the knife down on the table in front of me, but only because my arm is aching from holding it up for so long.

'I don't know, Alison,' he says, shaking his head. 'But killing a man and framing her for his murder is not the way.'

'It's the best I had,' I admit. 'And I didn't have much time to think about it.'

I'm faking the emotion of my impending death as a way to get Graham to relax a little and come closer, and it works. He moves towards the table, and I keep looking down until he tentatively retakes his seat. But the knife is still well within my reach and still just out of his.

'I'm so sorry for what Claire and I did to you,' he says. 'We were heartless, and you didn't deserve that. But Andy didn't deserve to die. And Claire doesn't deserve to spend the rest of her life in prison. That's too much.'

'Maybe. But what's done is done.'

'You can change it. You can talk to the police. So what if they arrest you? You won't go to prison. You'll just go to a hospital, and you won't have to serve out a full sentence.'

'Because I'll be dead in a few months?'

Graham looks like he doesn't want to confirm that's what he means, but he reluctantly nods.

'That may be true,' I say, reaching out and picking up his wine glass which still has some wine left in it. 'But I don't want to do that, and I certainly don't want to spend my last few days in some hospital while a policeman watches me take my final breaths. I want to die here. In my own home. Where I belong.'

I take a sip of the wine, and it really is making me feel better about what I am doing.

'Claire shouldn't be in prison for this.'

'You would like her to be free, wouldn't you? That would mean that you'd be able to pick up right where you left off together.'

'That's not what I'm getting at, and you know it.'

'Do I? I don't know anything about you anymore. You don't tell me anything, and when you do, I'm not sure if it's true.'

Graham seems to take that on board as he watches me finish his wine before he speaks again.

'The police aren't just assuming that Claire is guilty.'

That was unexpected.

'What do you mean?'

'She told them that somebody must have framed her and when they asked her who would have reason to do such a thing, she gave them your name.'

This really is unexpected.

'How do you know that?'

'Because the police told me when they spoke to me. They obviously have no evidence, but they are open to the idea that it might not be as cut and dry as it's been made out to be.'

That is irritating.

'If you kill me then it will really be obvious that you are the one behind all of this. Then Claire will walk free, and you'll be the prime suspect.'

'Not necessarily,' I say.

'Oh, you didn't hear the way those two officers asked me about you. They definitely have their suspicions.'

I think about that for a moment. If it's true, then I guess I didn't do a very good job of convincing them that I am a weak and feeble woman who isn't even capable of keeping her house tidy anymore, never mind killing a man in his own home. But suspicions are okay. Suspicions don't lead to convictions. Only hard evidence can lead to that.

'What are you going to do?' I ask my husband as I pick up the knife again and run my finger lightly along the edge of it. 'Save Claire or save me?'

Graham watches my finger running along the blade, probably imagining what it would feel like if I was to plunge it into him if he was to make an attempt to call the police tonight.

'Say I agree and keep quiet,' he says after a tense moment. 'How do you know I won't just tell the police when I'm out of the house where you can't get me?'

'I don't know that,' I say. 'That is a problem. But all problems have a solution.'

That's when I do the thing I have been building up to all day. The thing I have needed to get so much wine into my system for. The thing I have decided is the only way to take control instead of letting fate decide it for me.

I'm dying.

But that doesn't mean I can't choose how I die.

Without warning, I use the knife to slash two deep lines in my left wrist. Before Graham can react and take the knife from me, I do the same to my right wrist, and now the blood is pouring out easily all down my baggy dress and onto the floor beneath my chair.

'Alison! No!' Graham calls to me as I already start to feel weaker, and by the time that I have dropped the knife and he has made it to my side, I am already starting to slide out of the chair.

He helps ease me onto the floor, where the pool of claret has formed beneath my chair, and as he desperately tries in vain to stop the flow of blood from my wounded wrists, I feel a sense of calmness come over me because I know the end is near. Screw waiting around to die in a few months' time when my body is riddled with tumours, and my mind is wracked with pain. I have decided that I will take charge and go out on my own terms. But before I do, I need to get an assurance that my husband really does choose me over her.

'Promise me you will keep my secret,' I say to him, as he does his best to cover my wounds with his hands, applying pressure and trying to stem the sea of blood that almost looks like it is everywhere now.

'Promise me,' I say again, more urgently this time because I don't have long left.

'Alison, hold on!' he cries, still squeezing my wrists, but the fact that I don't even feel pain anymore lets me know that I'll be gone very soon.

'Promise me,' I say, pulling one of my hands away from his grip and grabbing him by his shirt collar. His smart navy-blue shirt is now ruined from all my blood that is going all over him.

'Alison, please,' he says, still fighting even though he must have realised now that it is futile.

'All you have to do is promise me,' I say. 'And keep your word.'

He looks at me, unsure but aware that his promise seems to be my dying wish.

'I promise,' he says, as my eyelids grow heavy and the light in the kitchen seems to be getting dimmer.

'You promise you pick me over her?' I ask him for final clarification, wondering if they will be my last words because I have very little strength now.

'I promise,' Graham repeats, and I hope he sees the light in my eyes when I hear it.

But that will be all he sees because then my eyes close, and try as I might, I can't summon the strength to open them again.

Is this it? Am I dead?

'Alison!'

No, I must still be alive because I can hear my husband's desperate pleas. I guess that means I have time to say one more thing.

'I love you.'

I'm glad I got to say it before I slipped away.

I'm just sorry I never had the chance to hear his reply.

34

GRAHAM

I must have stayed there on the kitchen floor for ten minutes with my wife's dead body in my arms, holding her even though I knew that she could no longer feel it. When I did eventually get up and leave her, I was able to get a better idea of just how much blood there was around her, as well as all over me. My shirt and trousers were covered in claret, as were my hands and arms, and I knew that it would be a traumatic experience when it came to washing it off later. But I couldn't do that without calling for an ambulance.

Slumping into the chair that I had just enjoyed the lovely meal in, my blood-soaked hands fumble for my mobile phone in my pocket. As they do, my eyes land on the various plates of food on the table. There are plenty of leftovers. Fajitas. Tacos. Even a couple of empanadas still up for grabs, which is surprising because they were always Alison's favourites, and she very rarely left one behind. But the sight of it all makes my stomach churn now, and I have the blood to thank for that.

Quickly averting my gaze down to my mobile, I try to navigate my way to the keypad so I can call the emergency services, but my screen is quickly covered in blood thanks to my dirty digits, and that doesn't do anything for my queasiness.

My heart is still hammering in my chest even though I'm barely moving, and I know that I'm not going to make much sense to whoever answers the phone because I'm breathing so heavy. I need to calm down and fast, so I reach out for the bottle of wine and glug half of it down, hoping that a load of alcohol will keep my panicked feelings at bay.

It doesn't do the job though, and I doubt anything will. My wife is still lying dead on the kitchen floor in front of me, and I'm still sitting here covered in her blood.

I haven't cried yet, but I guess that's because I'm in shock. I haven't screamed either but that could be for the same reason. All I can do is look at what is left of my marriage and feel an overwhelming wave of sadness for how it ended.

Alison's confession that she was the one who had murdered Andy should have been the most shocking part of this evening, but amazingly, even that admission had been eclipsed by what had happened next. I had thought that the knife was to be used on me, and Alison had certainly made it sound that way with her threats and with the way she had pointed it in my direction. But then she had stunned me by using the deadly weapon on herself, slitting her wrists and taking her own life, using her last few moments to make me promise her that I would not tell anybody about what she had done to Andy, effectively choosing her over my lover who remains in custody for the gruesome murder.

I had told my wife what she wanted to hear because how could I not? I couldn't deny a dying woman her last wish. But now she is gone, giving me more time to think about my answer to the question she posed tonight.

Would I choose her or Claire?

I chose Alison, but that was when she was still alive. Now she has gone, how could I not choose Claire?

I need more wine, and I need it now, so I get up quickly out of my seat and go for a fresh bottle from the rack. Opening it quickly, I swig from the bottle, having lost my sense of control after witnessing such a harrowing event.

The house is eerily silent, as it should be now that I am technically home alone. But I'm not alone. Alison is still with me, or at least her body is, and every minute that ticks by is an unsettling one, nothing more than a reminder that I really should have called the emergency services already because that's the right thing to do in a situation like this.

So why haven't I done it yet? Why is my blood-smeared mobile phone sitting on the table beside all the plates of Mexican food while I stand over here by the kitchen counter drinking wine straight from the bottle?

Is it because I'm scared of what will happen when I make the call? Yes, I am definitely afraid of speaking to another human being and telling them that my wife just committed suicide right in front of my eyes. But it's not just fear that is preventing me from dialling 999. It's confusion too. Confusion about what I am going to tell the police when they inevitably demand to know the full story of what happened here this evening.

I screw up my face as I refuse to slow down on the alcohol intake, demanding that my body takes the high volume of booze because that's the only way I'm going to stand half a chance of getting through the next couple of hours. The arrival of the paramedics. The grim looks on their faces as they confirm that Alison is dead. The bodybag. The police officers. The questions.

The urgent need for me to give some answers.

That's when the thought of Alison's parents flash into my mind, and I have to stop drinking then because the sickly feeling in my stomach demands it. How the hell am I supposed to break this news to them?

‘Hi, guys. Sorry to bother you at this time of night but I have some bad news, I’m afraid. Alison killed herself. Right in front of me, actually. Yes, it’s terribly shocking, I know. I’m sorry for your loss and for mine. See you at the funeral. Goodbye.’

I know there will have to be a lot more to it than that, but that is the gist of it, and I cannot handle a conversation like that yet. Maybe ever. Hopefully, the police can just break the news to Alison’s family for me.

The police.

What the hell am I going to tell them?

They will want to know why Alison killed herself, and even I’m not sure what the answer to that is. Is it because she was dying anyway, so she wanted to get it over with before she became truly ill and too weak to do anything about it? Is it because she killed Andy and wanted to depart this life before any possible consequences of that came back to bite her? Or is it simply because she wanted to prove to me how much she loved me and how much my betrayal had hurt her, punishing me with her last act by making me watch her take her last breaths as she died in my arms?

I don’t know what to say, but I have to decide quickly because the longer Alison is dead, the more suspicious this will begin to look when the emergency services do eventually get here. If they know that I held off calling them for a lot longer than I needed to, then they will start to ask even more questions, and I already have enough of them to deal with as it is.

I've just lost my wife.

I don't want to lose my freedom too.

But the number one decision I have to make before I do finally call for help is whether or not I am going to honour my last words to my dying wife. Am I going to keep her secret, or am I going to tell the police that she killed Andy, which would hopefully see Claire released from custody?

I promised Alison that I would choose her, effectively leaving Claire to spend the rest of her life paying for somebody else's crimes.

But where would that leave me?

I'd be alone. I'm a widow now. My wife has gone. I no longer have to take her needs into consideration. Instead, I could just focus on my own and what I need is companionship. If I can't have that with Alison anymore, then maybe I can still have it with Claire.

I'm still undecided as I put the bottle of wine down and return to the table, where I pick up my mobile phone and wipe the blood off the screen with a clean part of my shirt.

As I dial 999, I take a deep breath. As I hear the operator's voice at the other end of the line, I look away from my dead wife.

I know she is gone, but I still feel bad for what I am about to do.

35

CLAIRE

Forgive me for not being excited about the prospect of another meeting with my lawyer. That's because so far, it has only been bad news that has been forthcoming from her, so today's impromptu meeting must only be more of the same. She's already given me plenty of news before, like how much evidence the police had on me, or that I was being charged with murder, or most recently, that I had been denied bail and would have to remain in custody until my trial.

I can't wait to hear what cheery news she has for me today. What is it this time? The UK has suddenly agreed to the death penalty, and that is now the best outcome I can hope for? It might seem over-dramatic to think like that, but with the way my luck has been recently, then it might as well be the case. Everything that could go wrong has gone wrong for me over these last few months, from Graham choosing Alison over me to that bitch presumably framing me for the murder of my ex-husband. The problem is, the police don't believe me when I tell them I must have been framed, so

I'm stuck in here while Alison and Graham are out there living together and enjoying the company of each other.

To say I came off worst in this situation would be the understatement of the year.

As I am led into the room where today's meeting with my lawyer is scheduled to take place, there is a good reason why I have my head bowed and my shoulders slumped. I am defeated, worn out and fed up, and I really don't expect the next half an hour is going to do much to change my mood. But then I see the expression on my lawyer's face and realise that I might be wrong. That's because she is smiling, and one thing that I have learnt about my lawyer ever since I started paying her to try and get me out of this mess is that she never smiles.

Never.

'Hi, Claire,' she says to me as I reach the table where she sits.

I study the woman as the police officer behind me tells me to take a seat in the empty chair opposite her. My lawyer is a woman by the name of Deborah Oldham, and if she doesn't sound like some flashy and high-flying legal eagle, then she doesn't look like one either. She's in her forties but looks much younger, and with her mousy hair, baggy suits and tiny hands that always seem to be fidgeting, she looks more like somebody on work experience rather than a seasoned veteran in this line of work. But she is the best I could afford, although the expression 'you get what you pay for' has crossed my mind more than once since I started meeting her and found out she wasn't doing a very good job of getting me out of this mess.

But why the smile today? Why does she actually look happy to be meeting someone like me in a place like this?

'What's happened now?' I ask as I settle into the chair, already bracing myself for another unexpected development in my ill-fated case, even with the smile. In my paranoid state, I have already decided that the only reason Deborah is grinning is because she has had some good news in her personal life and is not professional enough to contain it. Maybe she has just been asked out on a date. Or perhaps she has just found out she is pregnant and will get to enjoy a long period of maternity leave outside of this dreary job. Whatever it is, it surely can't be anything that can help me.

Deborah sits forward in her seat, her diminutive figure looking even smaller today than it usually does, before she finally lets me in on the reason for her happiness.

'Alison Monroe is dead,' she says, her smile not really matching what most people would consider to be bad news. But then she qualifies it with something that definitely explains that grin of hers. 'She killed herself but not before confessing to Andy's murder.'

That's a whole lot of crazy information packed into two short sentences, and I initially have trouble processing it all. But Deborah has obviously already spent the morning processing it for me and wastes no time in explaining what this means.

'The police have to look into this and try to determine that it wasn't a false confession, but from what I'm hearing, it seems Alison might be their woman, which means you will no longer be on the hook for Andy's death.'

Wow. That is good news, mainly for the fact that I had absolutely nothing to do with my ex-husband's death. But wait. Alison is dead?

'She killed herself?' I ask, struggling to imagine my ex-best friend doing such a scary thing.

'Yes, slit her wrists right in front of her husband, I believe.'

Oh my. I wonder how Graham is doing. Then again, I shouldn't be thinking about him because he wasn't thinking about me when he decided to go back to his wife.

'Why would she do that?' I ask, trying to fathom this.

'I don't know exactly. Could be guilt. Could be because of her terminal diagnosis. The police are still speaking to Graham to try and get all the facts, but I thought I'd let you know the news as soon as possible so you know that there is a good chance you will get out of here.'

'When?'

'I don't know yet. Bear with me. I'm working on it.'

I nod my head, but I'm still confused. Why would Alison confess and give me a chance to get out of here? I was obviously right about her being the killer and framing me, which is crazy enough, but now she has just killed herself and given me a ticket to freedom. Why?

It's a shame she isn't around anymore to ask.

Deborah runs through what will happen next, but I struggle to hear most of it because my head is swimming with all sorts of thoughts about Alison, Graham and the fact that I may very well be a free woman again. But I also think about Andy and how Alison came to be in his home that night she killed him. How did she get in there? I really hope Alison has explained everything to somebody somewhere before she died, otherwise there's a lot of unanswered questions I'll always have rattling around in my head.

But the main thing is that I am getting out of here, or at least I should be unless my lawyer botches it up.

'Just do what you have to do,' I tell her as our meeting comes to a close. 'Don't let the police mess this up or keep me here a second longer than I should be.'

Deborah nods her head, and as has been the case for a while, my fate rests in her tiny hands again.

As she says goodbye to me and urges me to keep going because it will all be over soon, I think about smiling at her like she smiled at me when I entered, but I decide against it. That's because smiling is for happy people, and I'm not happy. Not yet, anyway. I won't be happy until I get out of this place and for the time being, I am still stuck here. But things are definitely looking better now, and if all goes well, I could be a free woman very soon, able to enjoy all the things that come with that.

Walking in the park. Getting my hair done in a salon. Drinking wine on a Saturday afternoon. Falling asleep on the sofa while watching a rubbish movie. All the standard things that I used to do and so many other people do too, the things we all take for granted. Soon, I may get to do them all over again.

I cannot wait.

But I still have an unsettling feeling in my stomach as the police officer leads me away from the room where diminutive Deborah still sits. It's a feeling that tells me something might still be wrong, and that's because if I have learnt one thing about Alison Monroe in all my time of knowing her, it's that she never does anything without having a good reason to.

So if she has just done something to help get me out of prison, then she must have a damn good reason why and I worry that it has a lot more to do with simply doing the right thing and allowing an innocent woman to walk.

She has given me an avenue out of here by telling Graham what she did.

But why?

Even though she is dead, I still feel like Alison might be playing with me and the man I cheated on her with.

36

GRAHAM

I've had the grim experience of making funeral arrangements before when both my parents passed away within a year of each other. But it's a slightly different experience this time now that I am doing the same thing for my wife. Unlike my parents, who had both been in their late eighties, Alison was only forty, and that is certainly not an age when people should be getting buried. But that's what must happen now after poor Alison cut her wrists right in front of me and died on the kitchen floor of the home we shared together.

The police have conducted their investigations and are satisfied that it really was suicide, and I'm glad there were no questions for me about why I took a while to call for the emergency services after my wife died. I assume they must think that I called as quickly as I could once the initial shock had worn off, and that's almost the truth, so I can live with that. What is harder to live with is the fact that I have broken my word to my dying wife and cancelled out what would have been her last wish.

Alison made me promise her that I would choose her over Claire, and to do so would have meant that I kept what my wife did a secret and allowed Claire to go down for Andy's murder. But I decided I couldn't do that, although my reasons for reaching that decision were not entirely about doing the right thing for justice. While it would have been extremely difficult to see Claire sentenced to a life term behind bars when I really knew the truth, it would also have been extremely difficult for me to have lost both women and ended up alone. At least this way, with Claire's release now believed to be just a matter of time, I have a chance of reconciliation with one of the women in my life. Hopefully, Claire and I can still make things work, and the fact that I have provided the information that should help her regain her freedom means that I have earned some serious brownie points there. But I won't know for sure until I see Claire face to face, and that won't happen until she is out. That's because I'm not going to make any kind of effort to get in contact with her or visit her while she is still in custody because I don't want the police to get suspicious and think that I somehow concocted Alison's confession just so I could get back the woman I really love.

But that is unlikely, based on the evidence Alison left behind to prove that it was really her who killed poor Andy. Along with the handwritten note in which she detailed her crimes in such a way that only the killer could have known, there is also the presence of the knife with Andy's DNA on it which was in a small box in the spare bedroom just as Alison said it was. That means the police are confident that my wife was the killer, although it also means the funeral is going to be a very strange experience for all involved when it comes around. That's because I'm not sure how many people are going to feel comfortable going to pay their respects to a woman who it has since emerged had committed a heinous crime before she passed.

Regardless of that knowledge, I will be there at the service, dressed in my black suit and assisting the other pallbearers with the movement of the coffin that contains her body. That's because she was my wife, and despite what she did and all the things we went through together, I still love her and want to respect the memory of her on the day she is laid to rest. I will also be making a short speech at the service, nothing too wordy but just something for the attendees to take away from the day. I will speak about Alison as I used to know her. The bubbly, bright woman, who gave so much and still had so much to offer before she was cruelly diagnosed with a disease that has taken far too many before their time. I won't mention what happened after that, for obvious reasons. Instead, I will be making sure to wrap it up with a cheery memory of the woman who was my wife. It will be emotional, and it will definitely be awkward, mainly because I know there will be many people who will have heard the rumours about me cheating on Alison with the woman she ended up framing for murder, but I will just have to deal with that because the day won't be about me.

It will be about Alison, as it should be.

But part of me also acknowledges that the reason for my determination in putting on a brave face, making a speech and helping carry the coffin to the hole where it will lie for eternity is the fact that it will hopefully alleviate some of the guilt that I feel about betraying her last words. Maybe if I can give Alison the best send-off possible, then somehow, someway, wherever she is now, she will forgive me for breaking my promise and allowing Claire to get off the murder charge. But I realise that in reality, there is nothing I could do that would ever make up for me breaking that promise to my wife.

Deciding to keep busy so I can distract my mind, I return to the task in front of me. There are a few more things I need to do before the funeral, including several phone calls I need to make to various friends and family members. Based on my experience so far from the people I have already spoken to, the conversations will be a mixture of awkwardness, sympathy and shock.

Forgive me if I hesitate to pick up the phone and start dialling.

But dial I must because once this is done, the funeral can go ahead and the sooner that happens, the sooner my late wife is laid to rest. While it is a tragedy that she will never get to grow old like so many other people do, it is also a pleasant thought that she will remain eternally youthful, the image everybody has in their minds of her one that is never clouded by grey hair, wrinkles and a worn-down body. I decide that I will say that in my speech, hoping that it will provide some comfort to the people who are listening to it, particularly Alison's mum and dad, who are going through an unimaginable hell that only the parents of a deceased child can ever know. I doubt it will make up for the fact that Alison is dead, and I wasn't the best husband in the world, but it's an honest attempt at doing something nice for her.

The last nice thing I can ever do for her.

The feeling of guilt is coming on strong again as I see the vision of Alison's face as I held her in my arms just before she closed her eyes. 'Promise me,' she said and promise her I did.

I pick up the phone and start dialling before I feel any worse about breaking that promise.

37

CLAIRE

It's good to be home. It's even better to be here after the possibility of spending the rest of my life in a cell that is even smaller than my en-suite bathroom. But now I am home, and I can start to work on moving past the traumatic events of the last few months in which I was framed for murder by a bitter ex-friend.

I guess I have won and not just because I have my freedom. It's also because that bitter ex-friend is being buried today, meaning there is no more chance for revenge on her part. Even a woman as resourceful as Alison can't rise up from the grave and have the last laugh anymore. But it has taken me a while to realise that and feel comfortable about it. My paranoia about all of this still somehow being a part of Alison's twisted plan took a while to leave me, even when I was officially released and told that I was a free woman. But the more time that passes since her death, the more I feel confident that Alison's final act on this earth was not one of continuing revenge but rather just a way of absolving her guilt before she died.

With that in mind, there is no reason why I shouldn't put all my focus now on the important task of getting on with my life. That daunting prospect has been made easier by the fact that my employer has kindly kept my job open for me so I can return to it. They told me that their company policy had been to believe me and support me right up until the moment a guilty sentence had been handed down, and fortunately, that never came. With my job to go back to, that means money won't have to be a worry, and I'm grateful for that because I've had more than enough worries to trouble me lately.

So that's my professional life taken care of. Now there's just the small matter of my personal one to rebuild too.

Needless to say, romance has been the last thing on my mind ever since I found out my ex-husband had died and the police were looking in my direction. Even now that I am free, I still haven't entertained many thoughts about a new relationship.

But somebody else has.

Graham came to my house yesterday, clearly eager to see me after my release and the bunch of flowers in his hands only reinforced that. The silly grin he wore on his face when I opened my front door and saw him standing there told me that he must have expected me to welcome him in with open arms and thank him for helping me get out of the hell I have been trapped in thanks to his late wife. But of course, I didn't do that. Instead, I just slammed the door in his face because after what I've been through, it's going to take a lot more than a bouquet of cheap flowers to make me even want to listen to that man for more than ten seconds.

I still have some feelings for him, and I suspect those feelings will never truly go away, but in the same way, I will never be able to fully get over the fact that when it came to the crucial moment for him to choose between Alison or me, he chose her. That is a choice that we all had to live with, and I continue to live with it to this day. It's the reason why I am alone in my house now instead of sitting with Graham. He could have been with me every hour of the day now if only he had left his wife sooner like I had asked him to. I wonder if we could have avoided all of this if he had just done as I said. Instead, he's out there now on his own, and so am I.

I check the time and see that it is almost two o'clock. Alison's funeral is due to start in a few minutes, according to what the notice said in the newspaper, and I think about all the mourners making their way into the service, all dressed in black and all wearing glum expressions. I also think about Graham and how he will be there somewhere, dressed in a black suit and probably shaking a few hands and thanking people for coming. I wonder how sad he looks on the outside and whether or not he is actually sad on the inside where it really counts. I wonder if he is truly grieving for the loss of his wife or if he is just keeping up appearances.

I wonder if he still loves her or if he genuinely wants to get back with me like the bunch of flowers and the soppy smile on my doorstep suggested.

Who knows, and right now, who cares? I'll let him get on with burying his dead wife while I get on with what I need to tick off my to-do list today.

Entering my bedroom with a roll of bin bags in hand, I open my wardrobe and start taking out any items of clothing that I no longer wish to wear. This is usually called spring cleaning, but for me, it's more than that. After my experiences, I want a completely fresh start, and one way to do that is to rid myself of many of my old clothes so I can make room for the new.

Tossing items into an open bag with only the slightest of regard for how nice they are or how expensive they might have been, I am aware that I might not be behaving as rationally as I could be but screw it. It feels good to throw things away, and the more I do it, the more it feels like I am throwing away my past too. I want to forget about Alison and my dead ex-husband, just as much as I want to forget about all the long nights in police custody and all the tedious meetings with my lawyer as she fumbled about and tried to figure out something that might get me out of there. I also want to forget about all the tears I cried when I thought that my life really was over and that all I had to look forward to for the next twenty to thirty years was the erosion of my worth as a human being. And the final thing I should want to forget about is Graham, the man with whom I embarked on an affair with, an affair which caused all of that other stuff to happen.

So why can't I forget about him? Why do I keep thinking about him and how he might be feeling right now? Why does this black bin bag in which I am throwing all my clothes into also make me think of the black suit he will be wearing as he stands beside his wife's coffin and prepares to say goodbye?

I stop what I am doing and pick up the bin bag, deciding that I have made enough hasty decisions for one day and will give myself a chance to simmer down before I throw any more of my possessions away.

Carrying the bulky bin bag downstairs, I do my best not to lose my grip on it before I can get it outside and put it into one of the bins. I know the right thing to do would be to donate these second-hand clothes to charity now that I no longer want them, but that would require me driving down to the charity shop on the high street, and I don't feel like doing that anytime soon.

Opening my front door, I step outside and feel the warm sunshine of a clear day on my skin as I head towards the bins down the side of my house. It's a slight struggle to lift the bag high enough to drop it inside the bin, but I manage it before turning back to my door and preparing to go inside and make a drink. But before I can, I spot the woman standing on the pavement across the road, opposite my house.

While I don't recognise her, she seems to recognise me, but not in a way that means she is waving or smiling at me. It's in the way she is simply standing and staring at me, as if she knows who I am and is here to get a good look.

I stop by my front door and stare back at the woman, expecting her to say something that might help me understand why she is just watching me and my home. But she doesn't. Instead, she just walks away quickly down the street.

'Hey!' I call out after her, but she doesn't look back, and ten seconds later, she has disappeared around the corner.

Who was she? Why was she watching me? And will I see her again?

I have no idea, but as I close my front door and lock it quickly, that gnawing wave of paranoia has returned to me again.

On the day Alison is being buried, why do I feel like this has something to do with her?

38

GRAHAM

Burying my wife was tough. The service was long, emotional and draining for all involved. But now that Alison has been laid to rest, life, as they say, goes on. With that in mind, I have put on one of my best suits, applied a little aftershave and accepted the invitation for dinner that was extended to me earlier today.

To say I was surprised when Claire called and asked me to meet her at the local Italian restaurant this evening would be an understatement. After all, the last time I had seen her had been when she had slammed the door in my face after I had turned up on her doorstep with a bunch of flowers. But I was only too glad to agree to her request to go for a meal, and here I am now, looking good, smelling great and feeling like everything is going to be okay after this craziest of years so far.

But then I walk into the restaurant and see Claire sitting by herself at the table in the corner, and the look on her face tells me she might not be as excited about this evening as I am. As the maître-d shows me to the table, I hope that I have been wrong in my reading of her body language from across the room and that she will look livelier when I reach her. But my arrival at the table does little to change the look on her face, and as I thank the restaurant employee and take my seat, I have no idea what this meeting could be about. I had assumed it was because Claire was willing to make another go of things between us. But I'm guessing not.

So what is it?

'Are you okay?' I ask her as I watch her take a thirsty sip from her glass which looks like it contains just lemonade, but I suspect there is a shot or two of something stronger in there as well.

'Not really,' she replies when she has finished drinking. 'I feel like I'm being watched.'

'What do you mean?'

I glance around the restaurant to see if she is referring to anybody watching her right now, but it's early, and the venue is quiet, barring one couple in the other corner who are definitely not watching her or me.

'I saw a woman outside my house yesterday,' Claire says. 'She was just standing there and staring.'

'Who?'

'I don't know who she is. But it felt like she knew me.'

'Did she say anything?'

'No, she just walked off.'

'Well, it was probably nothing then. She might have been lost.'

Claire shakes her head.

'She wasn't lost. She seemed to know exactly where she was going.'

'Okay. It doesn't mean it's anything to worry about.'

'I saw her again today. When I left my office at lunchtime to go and get a sandwich. She was across the street from the car park. She was watching me again.'

I frown because this does sound very strange, and I'm not really sure what the explanation could be, but I doubt it is anything to worry about.

'She might have you confused with somebody else,' I suggest with a shrug.

'What if it has something to do with Alison?' Claire replies, and that was not what I was expecting.

'What?'

'What if this is her? She might have arranged for somebody to come and hurt me before she died.'

'Why would she do that?'

'Because of what we did together.'

'But it's over now.'

'She framed me for murder!'

I wince as Claire's loud voice catches the attention of the other people in here, and I imagine that's not the kind of statement a person expects to hear when they come out for a meal after work. Then again, I wonder if these people recognise Claire. After all, it wasn't so long ago that her face was plastered all over the news in connection with Andy's murder.

Then I realise that might explain why Claire feels like she is being watched.

'It could be somebody who saw you on the news,' I say, nodding my head as if to show that must be the explanation. 'They might have followed you out of curiosity or something. Like a fan following a celebrity.'

'Like a stalker?'

'I don't know about that.'

'I'm just so on edge,' Claire admits before reaching for her drink again. 'I feel like something is still wrong, even with Alison gone.'

I watch Claire drain her drink, and it reminds me of how Alison drank mine just before she slashed her wrists and bled to death in front of me. But surely I don't have to worry about something like that happening to me again.

'I'm sure it's nothing to worry about. But if you see her again, then maybe you could mention it to the police and let them look into it.'

'I'm not going to the police! Are you mad?'

‘Keep your voice down,’ I say, aware that the other couple in the room are looking over at us, and I’m starting to worry that we might be asked to leave. That won’t be conducive to the romantic meal that I was hoping to enjoy with Claire tonight.

‘I can’t believe you would even suggest speaking to the police after the way they treated me.’

‘They were just doing their job.’

‘But I was innocent!’

‘Yes, I know that, but it didn’t look that way at the time, did it?’

‘Thanks to your wife!’

I take a deep breath and reach out for Claire’s hand, hoping that I can calm her down by taking hold of her and making her realise that she is getting all worked up over nothing.

‘Look, I’m sure this is nothing to worry about. But if you see this person again, let me know, and I’ll see what I can do to make them stop.’

‘You’d like that, wouldn’t you? Being my protector? But where were you when I really needed you? Where were you when I was in custody? Shacked up with your wife, that’s where!’

Claire has really overdone it on the volume now, and I see the maître-d making his way over to us, no doubt to give us a warning about keeping the noise down, or he will have to ask us to leave. But I give him a wave to fend him off and let him know that it won't happen again, and it buys us a little more time because he stops and gives me a grumpy nod.

'Claire, you need to calm down, or they are going to throw us out,' I say, taking back my hand after not managing to get a grip of hers.

'Do you think I care about some poxy meal?' she hisses back. 'I just wanted to pick somewhere public to talk in case I was being watched again.'

'Oh,' I say, probably not doing a good job of hiding my disappointment.

'Wait. Did you think I had called you here tonight so we could get back together?' Claire asks me, shaking her head and obviously indicating how wide of the mark I have been.

'Well, I had hoped that was the plan,' I say.

'You're unbelievable,' she replies, and she grabs her handbag and stands to leave.

'Where are you going?'

'Home.'

With that, Claire walks away from the table, and I'm left with the choice of going after her and having an argument or sitting here on my own and ordering a meal for one while the maître-de and everyone else in here looks at me like I did something wrong.

In the end, I get up from my seat and go after Claire, catching up with her on the street just before she can get into a taxi.

'Wait!' I call to her as she opens the car door.

'What?' she hisses at me, and now it's the driver's turn to be subjected to our conversation.

'I don't want to leave things like this,' I say, being honest. 'I still think we can make it work.'

Claire glares at me, and I'm sensing that she doesn't agree. But just to ensure there is no doubt, she gives it to me straight.

'Leave me alone. I wish I'd never met your wife, and I wish I'd never met you.'

With that, she gets into the taxi and slams the door shut behind her.

As I watch the car drive away, knowing full well that I am never going to see Claire again, I feel a sense of loss wash over me. It isn't quite as profound as when I lost my wife, but it is as unexpected. Claire might not have left me as dramatically as Alison did, but she has still left me, and now here I am all alone, standing on a dark street.

Except I'm not alone.

There is somebody watching me from across the road.

I don't recognise the woman but I feel like I know who she is.

She is the woman Claire told me had been watching her.

Now she is watching me.

‘What do you want?’ I call out, but I get no answer, so I go to cross the road, determined to find out who this person really is and why they have such an interest in me and my former lover. Even if they are just a crazy person obsessed with the story of Andy’s murder and Alison’s suicide, they need to be told that they can’t just stalk either of us like this.

But I’m prevented from crossing the road quickly by a car coming down the street way too fast for the speed limit, and the holdup provides just enough time for the mysterious person to disappear around the corner.

By the time I have got across the street and rounded the corner, the woman is gone.

39

CLAIRE

I never used to double-check the lock applied on my front door before going up to bed, but I find myself doing it now. I know it's because of the mystery woman, and until I know who she is and what her intentions are, I can't be too careful. That's why I will double-check this lock, as well as double-check all the windows around the home are closed. They should be, but I have to make sure there is no way for anybody to get in should they come calling in the night.

This might be an indication that my paranoia is in overdrive now, but I think I have a right to be anxious. That's because it's not just me who has seen the mystery woman.

Graham has seen her too.

I was still in the taxi on the way back from the ill-fated meeting with my former lover when I saw that he was calling me. I avoided picking up, one because I'd said everything that I had to say to him before I left him and two, because I didn't want to subject the poor taxi driver to an argument. But I had no choice but to call him back once I saw the message come through from him in which he told me that he had seen a woman standing outside the restaurant who had obviously been watching our meeting this evening.

When I spoke to Graham, he sounded out of breath, and when I questioned him on it, he told me it was because he had attempted to give chase to the mystery woman to find out who she was and why she was following us. But he lost her, which meant we still had no answers. That's why I am now checking the lock on the door before I go upstairs to bed.

As I climb the staircase, my mind is buzzing with all sorts of crazy thoughts.

Is the woman dangerous? Is she after me, or Graham, or both of us?

And does this have something to do with Alison and the murder of Andy?

It's little wonder that as I walk into my bedroom and close the door behind me, I know full well that I am not going to be able to get a wink of sleep tonight. Taking off the clothes I put on to meet Graham at the restaurant, I feel slightly better now that I am wearing something more comfortable, although I had hardly been overdressed to start with. Unlike Graham, I hadn't made much of an effort for this evening, whereas he had obviously turned up at the restaurant treating the occasion like some weird kind of first date for us both again.

I don't feel bad about how bluntly I told him that we would never be together again because he didn't have any qualms about being brutally honest with me when he told me he was going back to his wife. But as I stand here now all alone in my quiet house, I can't help but feel like it might not have been a bad idea to string him along for a little while, if only to have some company until I find out who this woman is. Perhaps I was a little bit hasty with Graham because I sure could use the extra bit of protection that he would give me if he was here.

As I pull back the duvet and climb into bed, I think about calling him. I have no doubt he would be round in a flash if I asked him to come over. But as I hold my phone in my hand and settle into bed, I decide not to because it will only encourage him and give him the wrong idea. Having him around might make me feel better in the short term, but in the long term, I am better off having him out of my life so I can focus on what is ahead instead of what has gone before.

But the thought of me moving on and meeting somebody new one day is a little laughable because I hardly imagine there is a long queue of men out there just waiting to get with a woman who has been all over the news recently in connection with the brutal murder of an innocent man. The fact all charges have been dropped probably means little because once people associate you with something, it barely seems to matter whether you are innocent or guilty. The stigma follows you around regardless.

Therefore, I expect my days as a singleton are going to last a while.

Turning off the bedside lamp, I now only have the light from my phone's screen to provide me comfort from the spooky darkness. Still feeling wide awake and aware that is unlikely to change for a while, I decide to kill time by scrolling around endlessly on social media because what else is a person to do when they're lying in bed and can't sleep?

Thirty minutes looking at various people's pointless posts and celebrity photos that only make me feel envious of a better life perhaps unsurprisingly leaves me feeling worse than before I started, so I put my phone on silent and place it on my bedside table. Determined to give sleep a good go, I close my eyes and try to think about anything other than the fact that there might be a woman outside my house right now waiting to get another look at me.

Graham could be right. It might be some crazy person who has become obsessed with the Andy King case and all those connected to Alison. Hopefully, that is as sinister as it gets, and they will soon grow bored and leave me alone after realising that I'm really not as interesting as the newspapers had made me out to be.

But it's the thought that somebody might be out there now that makes it impossible to get any meaningful rest and the sound of the car door closing on the street outside only makes me jumpier. I decide to get up and go to the window to check outside and hopefully put my mind at ease that nobody is out there looking back at me. If there is, then I will take Graham's advice and call the police because, at the end of the day, I have done nothing wrong, so I shouldn't be afraid to seek their help.

As I get up, I pick up my phone, planning on using the torchlight on it to help guide me towards the window, so I don't stub my toe on anything on the way. But as I pick it up, I see the notification on my screen, and I drop the phone almost as if it was a hot plate I picked up by accident.

In the stillness and silence of my house, I can hear the thudding of my heartbeat as my brain processes what I just saw on my phone.

I had a missed call.

And it was from Alison's number.

It takes me a moment to pluck up the courage to kneel down and try and find my phone on the carpet after I dropped it, but I can't see it in such little light, so I have to use the help of the bedside lamp. As soon as that is on then I am able to locate my phone, and I see it lying on its side against the wall. It must have bounced over there when it fell from my hand, and I'm not surprised it went that far because I certainly dropped it quickly enough.

Picking it up, I look again at the screen, hoping that I just got confused in my drowsy state and imagined that Alison had tried to call me. Or even better, I actually managed to fall asleep, and now this is just a dream.

But it's not.

The missed call from Alison is still there.

Taking a deep breath, I unlock my phone and click on the dead woman's number, almost in disbelief that I am going to call a person who was buried only a few days ago. But before I can, I hear a loud crash from downstairs, and it sounds as if somebody has just kicked my front door in.

Running out of my bedroom, I look down and see that is exactly what has happened. My front door is smashed to pieces and is now wide open, allowing all the warm air to seep out of my house into the cold, dark night. But that's not all I see. I also see the police officers rushing through the open door, and several of them are coming upstairs towards me.

My phone falls to the carpet again, but this time it is because my hands are being forced behind my back, and handcuffs are being wrapped around my wrists.

I never did get a chance to call the number back.

I never did get to find out why I had a missed call from a dead person.

40

GRAHAM

After the drama of the argument with Claire and chasing the mysterious woman down the street, I hadn't gone home last night. Instead, I had found myself in some grimy pub drowning my sorrows, which I could be forgiven for doing after the recent passing of my wife. But it wasn't Alison who was on my mind as I sat there in the dreary bar sipping cheap lager and looking at all the posters for the various bands that had played in this dodgy venue over the years. Nor was I thinking about Claire or the woman who had been watching us outside the restaurant.

Instead, I was thinking about myself and how much of a mess I had made of everything.

My marriage. My affair. My life. All had ended in complete shambles, and I had nobody to blame for that but myself. It was that realisation that had seen me stay at that bar until closing time, the ungodly hour of two o'clock in the morning, before I had eventually been asked to leave. But even then, I hadn't gone home, instead checking myself into the 24/7 bed and breakfast that was conveniently situated just across the road from the pub, as if it knew there would be plenty of potential customers flooding through the doors after a night spent drinking in that place.

I had managed to find enough cash in my pocket to pay for a room for the night before staggering up the rickety staircase into the tiny bedroom I had purchased for the evening. As I had collapsed onto the bed and closed my eyes, I wondered where I ranked on the scale of degenerates who had slept in this room over the years.

Adulterers. Addicts. Desperate people with nowhere else to go. Was I any better or any worse than any of them? I hadn't stayed awake long enough to find out.

By the time I woke up, bright sunlight was streaming through the flimsy piece of material that I presumed was supposed to pass for a curtain, and I had quickly got up and gathered my belongings before checking out and going in search of a place to buy breakfast. A greasy spoon café had also been conveniently located at the end of the street that housed the dodgy pub and the even dodgier hotel, and it was almost as if all of man's basic needs could be met in this one small street in this rough end of town.

But not even a hearty breakfast of eggs and bacon had done much to lift my mood, and that's because I knew that not all of man's needs could be satisfied by cheap alcohol, greasy food and a place to lie down at the end of the day. I had another need, and I knew it couldn't be met around these parts. It was the need for companionship. That feeling of being needed by another human being.

The feeling of being loved.

With both Alison and Claire no longer in my life, I was feeling lonelier than ever, which was why I was determined to make the most of yet another day out of the office on compassionate leave and continue my drinking. That is how I ended up back at my local golf club, sitting in the member's bar and supping another pint of bitter poured by the pretty barmaid who served me in here the last time I played a round. But there was no golf today because I hadn't bothered to go home and get my clubs. Instead, I'd just taken a taxi from the town centre straight here and carried on my drinking. I had no idea how long I was going to stay for, and I wasn't sure when I was going to finally go home, but for the moment, I'm determined to stay out as long as I can.

Anything to put off going back to that empty house and having to face the reality of what my life looks like now.

As I take another sip of my drink, I take my phone from my pocket, hoping to find some entertainment on there to keep me company in the absence of an actual drinking buddy, but the screen is blank, and my button-bashing does nothing to change that. The battery must have died, which is hardly surprising considering that I haven't put any charge into it since before I left home to meet Claire at the Italian restaurant yesterday.

Lifting my weary body out of my seat, I shuffle over towards the bar and smile at the woman behind it as she absent-mindedly polishes a wine glass.

'You haven't got a phone charger by any chance, have you?' I ask, only slurring my words slightly, which I feel is a decent accomplishment considering how much I've been drinking since I got here.

'Yeah, you can use mine,' the barmaid generously offers, and I take it from her and plug it into the wall by the bar, meaning I can stand there and check it before I return to my table.

As my phone gets new life and turns itself on, I gaze longingly at the barmaid as she goes back to work, but I end up staring for too long and she catches me, smiling awkwardly before walking away and disappearing into the back room.

She probably wants a break from me.

Just like every other woman I've been with.

Fortunately, my phone is now useable, and I am able to distract myself with all the messages and emails that have accumulated on there since I last used it. There's plenty of texts from people offering me their condolences after hearing about Alison, even though it has been a while now since she passed. Either some people are very slow to catch up with the news, or they have just been lazy and taken their time in sending me a message of support. But better late than never, I suppose, and at least these texts remind me that I'm not as alone as I think I am.

I'm just about to go into my emails and see if there's anything of more interest in there when I notice that I have a new voicemail message. It's funny because I was in this clubhouse the last time that I had one of these. That time it had turned out to be the police who had been trying to get in touch with me, but I really hope it's not them again. I've had enough of men in black and white uniforms for one lifetime.

I click the new message and put my phone to my ear, and if I had to guess, I would predict that this voicemail is going to be from another well-wisher who couldn't make it to the funeral and has decided that a brief call is enough to make up for that.

But I'm wrong. It's not a well-wisher.

The voice on the phone now belongs to my dead wife.

'I knew you were going to choose her,' Alison says as I grip the edge of the bar. 'I hope you and your murdering lover are happy together.'

Then the message ends, leaving me staring at my phone like it's some foreign object.

What the hell was that? A message from beyond the grave? Impossible. Yet it was Alison's voice, loud and clear, as if she was alive and well and I didn't just speak at her funeral earlier in the week. How could that be? The only way I can conceive is that it was recorded before she died, and somebody else has sent it to me in her absence.

But who and why?

And what the hell was that part about me and my murdering lover?

I regret asking for the phone charger now because I would have been much happier just staying at the table and drinking my pint in blissful ignorance of the message's existence. But now that I have heard it, I can't unhear it, and all the paranoia that Claire seemed to be riddled with last night now comes for me, leaving me sweaty and afraid.

The sound of the phone ringing behind the bar makes me jump, and I watch as the barmaid reappears and goes to answer it. I keep my eyes on her as she speaks to the person at the other end of the line for no other reason than because she is a comforting sight at a time when I feel more stressed out than I have ever been before.

But then I notice the barmaid glance towards me with a troubled look on her face, and while I don't hear everything that she says, I do hear one bit of it.

'Yeah, he's here.'

Is she talking about me? She is looking right at me, so I have to assume so. But who could be calling for me here?

The barmaid is still on the phone, although she isn't saying anything else, nor is she looking in my direction. But I sense that the call is about me, and I also get the sense that I should leave here sooner rather than later.

Taking the charger out of my mobile, I leave my half-finished pint on the bar and walk away.

'Hey, Graham. Where are you going?'

Normally, I would be thrilled that a pretty barmaid sounded sad to see me leaving but not now. The fact she just shouted after me makes me even more convinced that the person on the other end of that phone call is asking about me and my current whereabouts.

I push through the clubhouse doors that lead into the car park, but it's at that moment that I remember I didn't come here in my own car. I came by taxi, which means my only way to leave here is to call another one.

I feel nervous, and my hands are sweating as I use my phone to call a cab, and I think how ridiculous it is because I'm not even sure what it is that I'm supposed to be running from. But the message from Alison has me feeling like something very bad is going to happen, and the barmaid watching me as she told somebody where I was only made me feel worse.

'Yes, taxi please. Higher Brow Golf Club. As soon as you can.'

The operator tells me that he will have a cab there in five minutes, and I guess that will have to do. But it's only two minutes later, as I stand there in the car park beneath the bright sunshine that isn't helping my hangover or my nervous disposition, when I hear the first sirens.

Thirty seconds later, and there are dozens of them.

Then I see the blue flashing lights of the police cars racing up the country lane towards the club, and even though I don't understand what this is all about yet, I just know that they are coming for me.

I consider running, but where would I go, and how can I ever hope to escape if I don't even know what I am supposed to be running from?

That's why I end up staying where I am as the cars arrive in the car park, and several uniformed officers get out of them and rush towards me.

I catch a glimpse of the shocked expression on the barmaid's face as she stands in the doorway of the clubhouse and watches me get hauled into the back of one of the cars, handcuffs around my wrists and the strong hand of a police officer pushing my head down.

I'm told that I am being arrested for the murder of Andy King, but that doesn't make any sense to me because my wife already confessed to that crime before she died. But I'm also told that anything I do say will be used as evidence, so I decide to stop talking and wait until I have a lawyer with me before I protest anymore.

As the car door is slammed shut behind me and the policeman behind the wheel puts our vehicle into motion, I have so many questions and very few answers. But the last thing to run through my head as we pull out of the golf club car park and back onto the country road headed for the station is the first thing that Alison said to me in her mysterious voicemail message.

'I knew you were going to choose her.'

It's as if Alison knows I lied to her as she lay dying in my arms. But how can she possibly know that?

I don't start getting answers until I get to the police station and speak to my lawyer and the investigating officers. But after that, I no longer have any more questions because my fate is clear as day.

I'm screwed, and so is Claire.

That's because Alison has won.

She has got her revenge on both of us.

And she has done it from beyond the grave.

EPILOGUE

ALISON

There's not much a dead person can do, which is why it's always better to put plans into place before you pass away. That's what I have done, and even though I won't be around to see them implemented, I know they will be carried out exactly as I wish, although I hope they don't have to be. That's because I will give my husband a choice before I die, and it will be his chance to avoid a nasty fate. If he chooses the right option, he will get to live out the rest of his years as a free man, going to work, playing golf and most likely meeting somebody new one day and settling down with them. But if he chooses the wrong option, then he will lose all his rights and privileges, and he will only have himself to blame for that.

I plan to kill myself during our Mexican meal tonight. I will do it by picking up a large knife and cutting my wrists, working fast and efficiently, so there is no chance of Graham stopping me, as well as no chance of me surviving my injuries. I'd much rather not have to die this way, but it seems it's a choice between taking my own life or waiting for the cancer in my body to take me, and I'd rather be the one to dictate the terms of how I go out. I wish I could grow old like so many lucky people are able to do, but I have been denied that opportunity by a cruel disease. At least this way, the disease won't kill me.

Instead, I will kill it.

It goes without saying that I'm nervous about what I am going to do tonight. I know it isn't going to be easy to go against human nature and mortally injure myself on purpose. The brain spends all of its time striving to keep the body out of danger, so to intentionally cause myself harm is to go against hundreds of thousands of years of human evolution. But it is what I must do if I am to give my plan the best chancc of working.

Hopefully, I won't chicken out at the last moment and will manage to make the requisite cuts on my skin that cause the blood to pour from my wrists and the life to quickly drain out of me. If so, I will only have one more job to do then before I die.

I will ask Graham to make me a promise. It will be a simple promise and one that any self-respecting husband should have no trouble agreeing to and adhering to. It will be to promise that he chooses me over the woman he cheated on me with.

His wife or his lover. Me or Claire.

Pick me, and everything will be fine.

But pick her and see what happens.

I expect he will say what he knows I am hoping to hear, promising me that he chooses me if only to give a dying woman her last wish. But he better hope for his sake that he means it, otherwise he is in for a shock, and it will be an even bigger one than witnessing me kill myself right in front of him.

One of two things will happen when I die. Either Graham will keep his promise and honour my last request, forgoing any feelings he might still have for Claire and leaving her to toil in police custody until a guilty verdict is handed down and she begins her life sentence for Andy's murder. Or he backtracks on what he will promise me and tells the police that it was I who killed Andy, giving Claire a chance at freedom which I am sure her lawyers will take, and allowing her out to potentially rekindle a romance with my husband.

I wonder what Graham will do. Sadly, I won't be around to see it.

But I know somebody who will.

I have paid a woman to keep tabs on my husband and his lover after I am gone. Her name is Kate, although I expect that isn't her real name because it would be best for her if she could never be tracked down and connected to all of this if things go wrong.

Her job will be a simple one.

She is to check if my husband has chosen me or chosen Claire.

If she sees Graham living alone while Claire remains in custody, then she will know he chose me. If she sees Claire released and Graham meeting his former lover, then she will know he chose her. If it's the first one, then Kate won't have much to do at all.

But if it's the second one, then she will have to get to work.

Assuming Graham has told the police of my guilt in order to get Claire off the murder charge, he will also have told them that I killed myself because of the guilty conscience and that the existence of the murder weapon and the note proves that I did it because otherwise, how would I know where the knife was?

But such a betrayal does not deserve to go unpunished, so if Graham is willing to stain my legacy and have everybody remember me as a murderer, then it's only right that I get my own back.

If Kate sees Claire released as a free woman, then she is to get to work, first maintaining visuals on both my husband and his lover before posting a letter to the police, written by me and explaining what has really happened.

The letter will tell the reader that I, Alison Monroe, took my own life not because of any guilt I felt over my involvement in the murder of an innocent man but because of my husband's involvement instead. I will explain that while it was Claire who killed Andy, Graham knew about it too, and when I found out, I was threatened and forced to keep the secret quiet until the cancer took me at the end of the year. But the threats and the burden of it became too much for me, and I took my own life.

That will give the police reason to think that Graham then took the opportunity to use my suicide to his advantage and say that I confessed to the killing, therefore getting Claire off the hook and allowing her back out so that they could continue their sordid affair together. The photos that Kate will take of the pair together if they do indeed end up meeting again will also be contained with this letter, adding further credibility to the idea that they pinned Andy's murder on me and used it as a way of getting the real guilty party out of prison.

But there will still be room for doubt at that point, and the police officers could be forgiven for not knowing who to believe between an aggrieved wife, a cheating husband and a backstabbing best friend. They might believe me, they might believe them, or they might believe none of us. But I need them to believe me so I will have one more ace up my sleeve. There will be one more item in amongst the letter and the photographs of Graham and Claire together. There will be a tape, and on it will be the recordings of Claire talking about some of the ways she wanted to kill her ex-husband, as well as the conversation between Graham and I when he answered all my questions about the affair.

I recorded it all secretly.

Why?

Because I knew about their affair before Claire told me about it on my doorstep.

I first found out that my husband and my best friend were seeing each other behind my back a year ago. I had finished work unexpectedly early, and while I had first planned to go home and get started on the housework, I had decided at the last minute to call around at Claire's house and see if she had the time for a catch-up. I knew she had the week off work, so I thought I might be lucky enough to catch her at home. I did catch her, although not in the way I thought.

I caught her letting my husband out of her front door at three o'clock in the afternoon.

Of course, there could have been an innocent explanation for that, so I did my best not to jump to any conclusions too soon. But I did decide to keep better tabs on Graham, taking the occasional bit of sick leave so I could see what he was really up to all day when I thought he was working from home.

That was how I saw him go back to Claire's house.

Again, and again.

And again.

There could be little doubt about an affair then, but there was still plenty of doubt about what I planned to do about it. I knew I should just leave Graham, but I was afraid. Afraid of losing him, afraid of losing my best friend too, and most of all, afraid of everybody knowing that I was one of those women who had allowed herself to be walked all over and betrayed by two people she thought cared about her. So I needed a plan. Until then, I had to act as if everything was okay. That meant pretending like Graham was the perfect husband, as well as acting like Claire really was my best friend.

I knew that I needed a way to get my own back that would leave me looking like a winner and not a loser. I needed revenge.

I just didn't know what to do.

Time went by, and the affair went on, and I was still no nearer to having a good idea. And then I found out I had cancer. That gave me further pause for thought. I still wanted revenge, but I also knew I didn't want to be alone at such a trying time.

But then I found out I was terminal. At that point, whimsical things like the fear of being alone or the frivolity of choosing what to do next go out of the window, and all that matters is that you make the most of each and every day while you still have the chance.

With my mind sharpened and my focus intensified, I lost the fear of being afraid, and I also figured out a good way to get revenge. And so the plan to kill Andy was born, framing Claire and leaving my husband without his lover, alone just like I was.

A lot has happened since then, and much of it unexpected, such as Claire admitting to the affair and Graham actually choosing to stay with me when he found out I was ill. I really had thought he would have just left me. But two things remained the same through it all. One, my need for vengeance, and two, the fact that time was running out.

As much as I have planned for it, I don't really know what will happen after I die. Maybe I've made mistakes, and Graham and Claire will remain free, or maybe the police just won't buy it and I will still be remembered as the most likely person behind the murder of poor Andy King. But I've tried my best, and I suppose that's all that really matters. We can all work as hard as we can to leave the legacy that we want to leave behind, but ultimately, we don't get to decide that because we're dead and we can't control how other people remember us.

If I could, I would want to be remembered as a strong woman who always did right unless she was wronged.

I think that's fair enough, isn't it? If not, then never mind. Life goes on, as they say. The problem is, we just don't know for how long. That's why I perhaps feel like there is a flaw in the writing of wedding vows. They are written in such a way that it's almost as if the people speaking them are able to see into the future and know that they will be able to stick to them no matter what happens. But that's ridiculous.

For better or for worse.

For richer or for poorer.

In sickness and in health.

It's easy to say those things, and it's easy to make those promises.

But it's also easy to break them.

Graham broke his vows, and, in the process, he broke me. Our wedding was ultimately pointless. But isn't everything pointless in the end?

By the time you read this, I will be dead. So what do I care?

I just hope there are no such things as wedding vows in the afterlife.

I'd hate for them to be broken again.

A Letter from the Author

Thank you for reading *The Broken Vows*. I hope you had as much fun delving into the lives of Alison, Graham and Claire as I had creating them. As with some of my earlier books, I wrote this during the lockdown period in England and it gave me a great form of escapism from the realities of the world. I hope it has done the same for you.

Without readers like you, I wouldn't be living my dream as a full-time author, so thank you for picking up this book and thank you for any review you may choose to leave for it afterwards. Reviews really are the most powerful way of getting attention for my books as they help bring in new readers. If you have enjoyed this book then I would be extremely grateful if you could spend a couple of minutes leaving an honest review on Amazon or Goodreads (it can be as short as you like).

Thank you and I hope you enjoy your next read,

Daniel

If you would like to get the latest news about my future books, receive free stories and learn more about the life

of a writer, you can join my e-mail list at
www.danielhurstbooks.com

Also By Daniel Hurst

TIL DEATH DO US PART

What if your husband was your worst enemy?

Megan thinks that she has the perfect husband and the perfect life. Craig works all day so that she doesn't have to, leaving her free to relax in their beautiful and secluded country home. But when she starts to long for friends and purpose again, Megan applies for a job in London, much to her husband's disappointment. She thinks he is upset because she is unhappy. But she has no idea.

When Megan secretly attends an interview and meets a recruiter for a drink, Craig decides it is time to act. Locking her away in their home, Megan realises that her husband never had her best interests at heart. Worse, they didn't meet by accident. Craig has been planning it all from the start.

As Megan is kept shut away from the world with only somebody else's diary for company, she starts to uncover the lies, the secrets, and the fact that she isn't actually Craig's first wife after all...

THE TUTOR

What if you invited danger into your home?

Amy is a loving wife and mother, to her husband Nick, and her two children, Michael and Bella. It's that dedication to her family that causes her to seek help for her teenage son when it becomes apparent that he is going to fail his end of school exams.

Enlisting the help of a professional tutor, Amy is certain that she is doing the best thing for her son, and indeed, her family. But when she discovers that there is more to this tutor than meets the eye, it is already too late.

With the rest of her family enamoured by the tutor, Amy is the only one who can see that there is something not quite right about her. But as the tutor becomes more involved in Amy's family, it's not just the present that is threatened. Secrets from the past are exposed too, and by the time everything is out in the open, Amy isn't just worried about her son and his exams anymore. She is worried for the survival of her entire family.

This will be one lesson they will never forget.

RUN AWAY WITH ME

What if your partner was wanted by the police?

Laura is feeling content with her life. She is married, she has a good home, and she is due to give birth to her first child any day now. But her perfect world is shattered when her husband comes home flustered and afraid. He's made a terrible mistake. He's done a bad thing. *And now the police are going to be looking for him.*

There's only one way out of this. He wants to run. *But he won't go without his wife...*

Laura knows it is wrong. She knows they should stay and face the music. But she doesn't want to lose her man. She can't raise this baby alone. *So she agrees to go with him.* But life on the run is stressful and unpredictable and as time goes by, Laura worries she has made a terrible mistake. They should never have ran. But it's too late for that now. Her life is ruined. The only question is: *how will it end?*

THE ROLE MODEL

She raised her. Now she must help her...

Heather is a single mum who has always done what's best for her daughter, Chloe. From childhood up to the age of seventeen, Chloe has been no trouble. That is until one night when she calls her mother with some shocking news.

There's been an accident. *And now there's a dead body...*

As always, Heather puts her daughter's safety before all else, but this might be one time when she goes too far. Instead of calling the emergency services, Heather hides the body, saving her daughter from police interviews and public outcry.

But as she well knows, everything she does has an impact on her child's behaviour, and as time goes on and the pair struggle to keep their sordid secret hidden, Heather begins to think that she hasn't been such a good mum after all.

In fact, she might have been the worst role model ever...

INFLUENCE

Would you kill for a million followers?

Emily Bennett dreams of being a social media influencer, just like her idols Mason Manor & Ivy Lane. But shortly after Ivy's untimely death she is contacted by a secretive businessman who offers her the chance at the fame and fortune she so desperately craves.

While Emily initially gets to experience the things she has always wanted, it soon becomes clear that her new employer had sinister motives for approaching her and it isn't long before she discovers that the life of her dreams comes with the kind of conditions that are the stuff of nightmares.

Social media isn't life or death.

It's more important than that.

THE 20 MINUTE SERIES

20 Chapters. 20 Characters. 20 intertwining stories.

An original psychological thriller series showing how we are all more connected to each other than we think.

<u>What readers are saying:</u>

"If you like people watching then you will love these books!"

"The psychological insight was fascinating, the stories were absorbing and the characters were 3D. I absolutely loved it."

"The books in this series are an incredibly easy read, you become invested in the lives of the characters so easily and I am eager to know more and more. Roll on the next book."

THE 20 MINUTES SERIES (in order)

20 MINUTES ON THE TUBE
20 MINUTES LATER
20 MINUTES IN THE PARK
20 MINUTES ON HOLIDAY
20 MINUTES BY THE THAMES
20 MINUTES AT HALLOWEEN
20 MINUTES AROUND THE BONFIRE
20 MINUTES BEFORE CHRISTMAS
20 MINUTES OF VALENTINE'S DAY
20 MINUTES TO CHANGE A LIFE

About The Author

Daniel Hurst lives in the North West of England with his wife, Harriet, and considers himself extremely fortunate to be able to write stories every day for his readers.

You can visit him at his online home www.danielhurstbooks.com

You can connect with Daniel on Facebook at www.facebook.com/danielhurstbooks or on Instagram at www.instagram.com/danielhurstbooks

He is always happy to receive emails from readers at daniel@danielhurstbooks.com and replies to every single one.

Thank you for reading.

Daniel

Made in the USA
Monee, IL
23 June 2021